THE HINGE OF LIGHT

BY DIVYA BABU

Clever Fox® PUBLISHING
Chennai • Bangalore

CLEVER FOX PUBLISHING
Chennai, India

Published by CLEVER FOX PUBLISHING 2025

ISBN: 978-93-6707-185-4

To my extraordinary family, whose love and support have been the bedrock of my life and work.

To my dear father, whose infectious passion for history ignited my spark. Countless evenings spent listening to your captivating tales of bygone eras have shaped my perspective and inspired my writing. Your unwavering belief in my abilities has been a constant source of encouragement.

To my incredible husband, whose unwavering support has made this dream a reality. Thank you for taking on the lion's share of parenting duties, providing unlimited cups of coffee, and offering invaluable feedback. Your patience and understanding have been instrumental in bringing this book to life.

To my beloved children, whose laughter and love have filled my life with joy.

To my beloved sister and mother, whose solid trust in me has fueled my journey. Your love, encouragement, and constant cheering have made all the difference.

To my father-in-law, whose voracious reading and encouraging words have significantly boosted my confidence and helped shape this book.

I dedicate this book to all of you, with heartfelt gratitude.

PROLOGUE

In the heart of ancient Greece, beneath the ruins of a once-great temple, a team of archeologists stumbles upon an ornate hourglass, intricately carved with scenes of gods and heroes.

Dr. Mira had come here for knowledge, for the thrill of discovery—but the stillness in the air, the strange sense of expectation, made it feel like the past itself was waiting for them.

Her thoughts drifted to the legend of Helios, the sun god, and the myth of his lost temple; whispers of a treasure hidden somewhere in the ruins. The Prism of Helios is a relic of unimaginable power, capable of altering the very fabric of time. Of course, most considered it a myth, a dream spun by ancient storytellers to explain the mysteries of the world. Yet, for some reason, Mira felt as though the truth was closer than anyone realized.

"Hey, Mira!"

Her attention snapped back to the present. Tony, her closest friend and fellow archeologist, gestured for her.

Mira walked towards him, her boots crunching softly against the gravel. As she drew near, she felt an unmistakable pull, a profound certainty that something lay hidden beneath the surface, a presence she sensed rather than saw. It was not a fragment of pottery, nor a weathered statue, but something different.

An hourglass.

The object was half-buried in the earth, its glass smooth and pristine despite its ancient surroundings. Intricate carvings spiraled around its frame, depicting figures she couldn't quite place, gods, heroes, or something else entirely. The golden sand inside shimmered in the fading light, swirling slowly as if moved by an unseen hand.

Mira didn't yet know the hourglass was linked to the Prism—two pieces of a mythic puzzle long thought lost.

Unbeknownst to them, it held the power to transport its bearer through time, weaving the threads of myth and history together. Their excavation, however, was driven by the legend of a lost temple of Helios, the sun god, said to guard the Helios Prism, a treasure of immense power that could hold significance in the modern world.

CONTENTS

Chapter One

Dr. Mira Kaelyn Ford

Dr. Mira Kaelyn Ford stood poised at the threshold of her dreams, a woman whose intellect and passion had long been defined by her love for archeology and ancient history. At thirty-two, she was a force of nature—a blend of determination, curiosity, and a deep-seated desire to uncover the mysteries of the past.

Growing up in a small town, Mira had always been captivated by stories of ancient civilizations. Her grandmother, a retired history teacher, filled her childhood with tales of heroes and gods, of epic battles fought and wisdom gained. Those stories ignited a flame in Mira, one that drove her to explore the world's ruins and unearth the secrets of those who came before her.

Mira's academic journey was a testament to her dedication. She earned her Ph.D. in archeology, specializing in ancient cultures, and her relentless pursuit of knowledge had taken her to various corners of the globe—from the pyramids of Egypt to the temples of Angkor Wat. Yet, it was Greece that held a special place in her heart, a land steeped in mythology and history that felt like the very Cradle of Western Civilization.

Mira's dedication to her work was matched only by her passion for teaching. She found joy in guiding her students, igniting their curiosity about the past, and encouraging them to think critically. Her mentoring style was hands-on and supportive; she believed that each student had the potential to make a lasting impact on the field. Her warmth and enthusiasm made her a beloved figure among her students, who often described her as both an inspiring teacher and a trusted confidante. Yet beneath her confident exterior, Mira carried the weight of loneliness. The demands of her career often left little room for personal connections. Friends were few, and her romantic life was virtually nonexistent. Mira yearned for a deeper connection, but the fear of vulnerability held her back. She often found solace in her work, pouring her heart into each excavation, hoping to fill the void with the thrill of discovery.

Though the world saw her as the brilliant, unshakable archeologist, there were softer corners of Mira that few ever glimpsed. She loved sketching ruins in her journal late at night, often by candlelight, letting the flickering shadows bring walls to life. Classical piano soothed her—she had taught herself to play as a teenager, fingers dancing over keys when words failed her. She collected old postcards too, from markets around the world, each one a glimpse into another's memory. Sometimes, after long days at dig sites, she would trace the inked handwriting with her thumb and wonder who had once written them—and who had waited to receive them. These small, tender rituals reminded her that history wasn't just in artifacts, but in people and the quiet lives they led.

Sometimes, in the quiet pauses between expeditions—when the adrenaline of unearthing the past faded, and the evenings stretched long and silent—Mira would find herself wondering. What if her path had been different? Would she have traded ruins for roots, sandstorms for steady hands to hold? Would there have been love, a quiet home, a life less transient? These thoughts came not with regret, but with a gentle ache—a kind of yearning that settled softly, like dust on an old photograph. They were echoes of a life not lived, tender and persistent, reminding her that even the most devoted seeker sometimes longs for the warmth of belonging.

A strong childhood memory emerged as Mira stood at the doorway to her newest excavation, unexpected yet welcome. She was eight years old and cuddled up on the floral-patterned couch in her grandmother's warm living room. The aroma of lavender and old books permeated the air, along with the subtle crackle of the fireplace. A book of Greek Mythology, with its vibrant and captivating drawings, was open on the tiny coffee table.

Her grandmother's voice, steady but laced with fascination, spun tales of gods and mortals. That evening, she recounted the legend of Helios, the Titan of the Sun, and his mystical artifact, the Helios Prism.

"They say, Mira," her grandmother had whispered conspiratorially, leaning closer, "that the Prism wasn't just a symbol of light. It was a key—a gateway to secrets hidden beyond the veil of time. Helios himself entrusted it to mortals once, but only to those deemed worthy." Flipping through the book's illustration, little Mira's eyes grew wide. The Prism was depicted as a flawless crystal, radiating a warm, golden light that pulsed gently, as if it held the very heartbeat of the sun within. Helios, his golden hair burning in the sunshine, lifted it high in his glowing chariot.

With her tiny hands following the Prism's outline on the page, Mira asked, "Has it ever been found?"

Her grandmother smiled, her eyes crinkling. "The destiny of the Prism has been lost to time. However, some claim it still remains, waiting for someone with a pure heart and unwavering will to rediscover it."

In the icy solitude of adulthood, that memory had lingered with her like a warm fire. Her grandmother's stories pushed her passion for archeology. Mira felt as though she was following in the footsteps of legends as she stood on the hallowed grounds of Delphi, where history and mythology were entwined.

She whispered to herself, "Maybe this is it, Gran," as the wind carried her words into the silence. "Perhaps this time I'll discover something that makes a huge difference."

As she stood on the brink of an excavation in Delphi, her heart raced not just with excitement but with the unshakeable feeling that this project could change her life. The potential for groundbreaking discoveries filled her with hope, and she could almost feel the pulse of history beneath her feet. This was more than just an excavation; it was an opportunity to prove herself, to embrace her passions, and perhaps even to find love in a place where myths came to life.

Little did Mira know that her journey would lead her beyond the realms of academia and into the embrace of ancient stories, where she would confront not only the challenges of time travel but also the depth of her own heart. As she prepared to lead her team into the unknown, she felt a whisper of destiny calling her, urging her to embrace the adventure that awaited.

✦ ✦ ✦

Chapter Two

The Excavation

The sun hung high over Delphi, casting a warm golden hue across the rugged landscape. Nestled at the foot of Mount Parnassus, the sacred site radiated an aura of mystery and reverence, drawing pilgrims and scholars alike for centuries. Today, the air was abuzz with the sounds of shovels striking the earth and enthusiastic discussion, echoing the excitement of discovery. Dr. Mira stood at the front of the excavation, her pulse pounding with adrenaline. As a seasoned archeologist, she had always desired or was born to discover the secrets of Delphi, the fabled oracle that once whispered prophecies to those brave enough to seek its wisdom. This magnificent setting, rich in history and mythology, provided the ideal backdrop for Dr. Mira to add to the heritage of a civilization that had influenced the path of history.

Mira looked around at her team, a diverse group of graduate students ready to leave their imprint, her eyes sparkling with determination. Joshua (Josh), her sarcastic but gifted student, was struggling to move a large stone block, murmuring humorously as he went.

Josh groaned, “Ugh, if we find a snake in here, I’m outta here for good!”

Mira just laughed and said, “Focus, Josh. If you find some treasure, maybe I’ll let you keep it.”

“Define ‘treasure,’” Josh shot back with a grin. “Because all I’m finding are rocks and... oh, look! More rocks!”

Nearby, Tony, her closest friend and fellow archeologist, was carefully brushing away dirt from a weathered artifact. He looked up, sharing his joy as his eyes glistened with anticipation. “Mira, check this out! I think this is part of an ancient Greek vase! This could be a big deal!”

Mira approached, kneeling beside Tony to examine the piece. The craftsmanship was exquisite, adorned with intricate designs that hinted at the cultural richness of the period.

“Incredible!” she murmured, turning the fragment over in her hands. “If we can find the rest of it, we might learn more about the trade routes of the era. Let’s make sure to document everything carefully.”

Annette (Annie), a lively art history major whose enthusiasm for Greek mythology provided an infectious energy to the group, and Jasper, a quiet but perceptive doctoral student with a talent for ancient languages, were others on the team.

Annie exclaimed eagerly, "And it could help us better understand the cultural context if this Greek vase contains any depictions of Dionysian rituals!"

Mira's mind raced with ideas as the sun started to set, illuminating the horizon with pink and orange shades. A window into the past, this location was more than simply a collection of ruins; it was a tapestry woven with the lives of visionaries, poets, and philosophers.

She felt an adrenaline rush when her shovel hit something hard.

Mira said, "Come on in, everyone! I think I found something!"

Her heart pounded as the others in her team came to her side, puzzled expressions on their faces. They unearthed the object together, gradually exposing the edges of a jeweled hourglass, its glass glittering even in the dimmest light. The base was decorated with intricate carvings of the sun and celestial bodies. At the top, there were symbols she couldn't immediately recognize, ancient and enigmatic.

Josh's eyes widened with wonder, he said, "Can you believe this? It's like something straight out of a legend!"

Tony, leaning closer, his voice filled with excitement, said, "This is incredible! Just look at those intricate carvings. They must tell a story!"

Mira's pulse quickened as she knelt, her fingers quivering as she swept away the dirt. The hourglass, with its cosmic symbols, appeared to shine with a heavenly brightness. She felt a rush of excitement mixed with a tinge of anxiety. Was this a sign? A message from the past? She couldn't shake the feeling that she was on the verge of something incredible.

Mira ran her fingers over the surface, instinctively tracing the symbols. Her fingers tingled with a sudden warmth, a sensation that made her stop. She had expected the glass to be cold, the stone of ages beneath it to be rigid and unyielding—but it wasn't. The hourglass seemed to hum with a soft energy, a subtle vibration beneath her fingertips.

"Strange," Mira whispered to herself. "This shouldn't be possible... these symbols aren't from any period I know."

Mira whispered to herself, her heart pounding. "This... this could be something truly amazing. We need to capture every detail. This could change everything we thought we knew about Delphi!"

Annie crouched next to her, brushing away dirt from the base. "This could be a lost relic, Mira. Maybe it's from Helios' temple."

Mira nodded, still studying the carvings. She had the inexplicable feeling that it was *calling* to her— almost as if it wanted to be touched, as if it had been waiting for this very moment. Her breath hitched.

Mira continued, "This isn't an everyday find. Check out the craftsmanship. The accuracy. It's just... otherworldly."

As the team gathered closer, the gravity of the moment began to sink in. Mira felt a buzz in the air, a physical energy that suggested they had uncovered something much more than an artifact. It was a bridge to a forgotten world, a gateway to untold stories.

But as she stared at the hourglass, an unsettling intuition flickered within her, a quiet whisper that hinted at adventures waiting just beyond her grasp. Little did she know, activating this artifact would unravel time itself, pulling her into a realm where gods and mortals intertwined.

As the team grew silent, Mira felt an odd pull, as if the hourglass itself was calling her to reveal its secrets. Her fingers moved instinctively, tracing one of the symbols. There was a subtle hum in the air, barely noticeable, but enough for her to pause.

Looking around, she asked, "Did you feel that?"

"Feel what?" Annie replied, her eyebrows raised.

"It seems to be vibrating," Mira murmured, her voice hardly audible above a whisper.

Josh stepped back, his face cautious. "Oh, Mira? Are you certain that it isn't cursed? Because I'm not planning to star in an ancient horror story."

Mira locked eyes with him, her voice firm yet reassuring. "It's our discovery, Josh. We owe it to ourselves to find out what it is."

Taking a deep breath, Mira strengthened herself to lead her team into the unknown, blissfully unaware of the life-altering journey ahead, one that would reshape her understanding of love, fate, and the very fabric of time.

"Mira," Tony said softly, "maybe we should document this and come back in the morning. We don't know what we're dealing with."

Mira turned to Tony. "Alright! Let's wrap up for now and continue tomorrow."

She turned to her colleagues and added, "And Jasper, let's get detailed photos from every angle and make rubbings of the inscriptions. Annie, see if there are any legends or myths that might refer to such an artifact."

"We have to secure the excavation site," Tony said. "Reinforcements will be required if this is as significant as I believe it to be."

The group nodded as their initial anxiety gave way to determined attention.

✦ ✦ ✦

Night Falls Over Delphi

Light from temporary floodlights softly illuminated the excavation site as the sun sank below the horizon. The group had pitched tents close by, and the sound of generators and the distant rustle of nocturnal creatures filled the air.

Mira sat by the artifact, alone, with her notebook open in her lap. Her detailed sketch of the hourglass included annotations for each sign she could recognize. But the more she looked at it, the more questions she had.

Why was it so deeply buried, hidden behind rocks and soil layers that indicated it had not been exposed to sunlight for thousands of years? What made it feel so... alive?

"Have trouble falling asleep?"

Tony's voice startled her. Bringing two warm mugs of coffee, he walked over and gave her one before settling down on the floor next to her.

She sipped and murmured, "Thanks."

"You've been staring at that thing for hours," Tony said, eyeing the hourglass.

"This could change everything we know about ancient civilizations," Mira said, her face warming as she glanced at him. "It's as if they were trying to tell us something, but we never knew how to listen."

Tony smiled faintly. "You always were the dreamer."

Mira countered, "And you were always the realist."

"Which is why we make a good team!" Tony said.

The weight of their revelation weighed down on them as they sat in peaceful silence for a while.

✦ ✦ ✦

Deciphering the Past

The atmosphere in their tent was charged with suspense. Laptops buzzed silently, their screens displaying study notes, images of the hourglass, and hastily scrawled translations. Everyone gathered in one of the tents, where

Mira spread out rubbings of the inscriptions along with ancient text samples retrieved by Jasper.

"This," Mira said, pointing to one of the rubbings with her pen, "is clearly tied to Helios. Look at the sun symbol that appears repeatedly."

While browsing a digital document on her iPad, Annie commented, "But Helios wasn't really part of Delphi's myths. The big name around here was Apollo. Everything was devoted to him, including the temple and the Oracle. So, what makes something associated with Helios buried here then?"

Tony relaxed back in his chair, arms crossed. "Maybe it predates the temple. Much earlier, as pre-Apollo worship. Civilizations periodically change their devotions, and deities go out of favor. What if this hourglass existed before Apollo's rule over Delphi?"

"That would make it extremely old," Jasper whispered almost to himself. He adjusted his glasses and focused on one of the artifact photographs. "But check out the craftsmanship, the attention to detail. This isn't archaic. Considering its estimated age, it is incredibly advanced."

"Then perhaps it's more than a relic," Mira muttered. Her words hung in the air, grabbing everyone's attention.

Josh raised his eyebrows. "Are you implying that it might be... workable?"

Mira was unsure as she replied. "I don't believe it's simply a symbol or some sort of religious thing. The hum we sensed earlier wasn't normal. And if the inscriptions are a code, they could be instructions or warnings."

More clues

As daylight broke, the team returned to the work site. Josh kept going with the digging, and it paid off.

With a flat, rectangular object coated in soil in his hand, he said, "I found this buried about six feet from where the hourglass was." He handed it to Mira, who gently wiped the soil away to reveal what appeared to be a metal plate with symbols similar to those etched on the hourglass.

As he knelt to inspect it, Tony proposed, "Could be a piece of a mechanism. If the hourglass works, probably this was designed to work in connection with it."

Running her fingertips over the plate, Mira said, "We'll need to analyze this back at camp. Annie, could you?"

As if in response to the plate's proximity, a faint, piercing sound began to emanate from the hourglass, subtly at first. Mira's fingers instinctively tightened around the plate, which vibrated faintly in her grasp, drawing her hand closer. The sound was faint at first, like wind flowing through a narrow passage, but it gradually became stronger, a deep, resonant hum emitting from the hourglass itself.

"Is that... from the artifact?" Jasper inquired, his tone a blend of curiosity and concern.

The team froze, staring at the hourglass. Instead of dropping in a continuous stream as it was when they initially dug it, the golden sand inside had begun to shift, swirling in slow, intentional patterns.

With caution, Tony said, "Mira, what is it doing?"

As she stared at the artifact, she said, "I don't know." She paused for a moment and continued, "But I think we're going to find out soon."

✦ ✦ ✦

Awakening of Power

As the sand began to swirl with greater force, the hum intensified into a low-frequency vibration that pulsed in their bones. Mira impulsively reached out with her hand hovering just above the hourglass.

"Mira, wait!" Tony shouted, but it was too late.

Before he could finish, an intense, blinding light burst from the hourglass as her fingers brushed a particularly intricate symbol. The world around her seemed to shift. The air thickened, the ground beneath her feet seemed to pulse, and an ethereal light surrounded the whole area. The glass shimmered with an unnatural, glowing radiance.

Mira was no longer kneeling in the ruins of Delphi. Instead, she stood in the center of a bustling marketplace, surrounded by people in tunics and togas, the air heavy with the scent of incense. The world around her felt... different. Alive in a way she hadn't expected.

Confused yet exhilarated, Mira stumbled through the marketplace, her senses overwhelmed by the sights and sounds around her. Just as she began to grasp her surroundings, she spotted her fellow colleagues, Joshua, Annette, Jasper, and Tony, trailing behind her, equally wide-eyed and taken aback.

"Mira?" Tony's voice was shaky. "What just happened?"

Mira gazed down at the hourglass. The sand had settled, but the artifact gleamed slightly, as if it had been charged with energy.

"I guess..." Jasper, dusting himself off, his voice shaky, "It activated."

Tony stood up. “Activated? What on earth does that mean? What did it do to us?”

Josh stretched his arms. “Oh Tony, maybe it teleported us to ancient Greece because that’s just what hourglasses do these days. Totally normal.”

✦ ✦ ✦

Chapter Three

A World Reborn

When Mira activated the hourglass, a bright light engulfed her, and she felt a surge of air, as if she were being pulled through time itself. When she eventually opened her eyes, she found herself in a bustling Delphi, alive with the noises of worshippers and the alluring aroma of incense. The distant clang of metal, the laughter of children, and the rhythmic chanting of priests all mingled in the air, foreign yet familiar. The streets were an infusion of vibrant energy and centuries-old traditions.

Around her, the others were just beginning to stir, blinking against the sunlight and trying to steady themselves.

A woman brushed past her in a flowing white and yellow robe with a pink floral pattern, its fabric whispering like silk in the breeze. The cloth was cinched at the waist with a braided cord dyed in deep indigo, and her bare feet moved gracefully across the dusty stone street. Balanced atop her head was a wide woven basket brimming with ripe figs, their deep purple skins glistening in the sun. As she passed, the thick, honeyed scent of the fruit enveloped Mira—earthy, sweet, almost intoxicating. She took a slow breath, letting the scent settle—a warm, sweet reminder that this strange world was undeniably real.

The aroma of honey-roasted almonds wafted from a nearby stall, curling through the air like a spell meant to lure wanderers closer. It was warm and nutty, with a touch of spice—perhaps cinnamon or cardamom—something distinctly ancient yet comfortingly familiar. Mira's stomach tightened with hunger she hadn't realized she carried, and for a moment, she was simply a traveler lost in time, drawn by the primal pull of food and fragrance. The air was rich—not just with history, but with life. It clung to her skin, filled her mouth, and wrapped around her thoughts like fine silk. Every breath was thick with the energy of a place undisturbed by modernity, where time moved to the rhythm of bare feet brushing against sun-warmed stone and vendors shouting prices in lyrical cadences. This wasn't a museum. It was the heartbeat of an ancient world.

The streets were lined with shiny limestone that glinted in the sunlight, giving the impression that Apollo's blessing was in the earth itself. The paths were lined with olive trees, their silvery-green leaves waving gently in the mild wind. Stall after stall formed a maze of vivid colors and tempting fragrances, selling everything from jars of golden honey to woven garments painted in hues Mira had rarely seen.

Though Delphi was not a coastal town, the breeze carried with it the faint tang of salt from the distant Gulf of Corinth.

The sound of street performers playing citharas and lyres blended with laughter and lively conversations that poured out from every corner. Amidst the bustle, a group of children laughed with joy as they chased a little goat adorned with flower garlands.

There was an aura of devotion in the air, and the Temple of Apollo, which towered over the colorful streets, threw a long shadow.

Annie muttered, looking around in confusion, "Is this really happening? It feels like we just stepped into a storybook."

Mira's eyes sparkled, her voice bubbling with enthusiasm. "This is absolutely amazing! Just look at all those vibrant colors! I can feel the energy buzzing all around us—it's like the city itself is alive!"

Jasper adjusted his glasses, eyes scanning the surroundings. "And the architecture! This is a goldmine for our research. Just imagine what we could learn!"

Tony grinned, his voice filled with enthusiasm. "Guys, we're actually in ancient Delphi! This is beyond anything we imagined. We have to soak it all in!"

Mira's mind raced, trying to process what had just happened. *This is impossible*, she thought, but deep down, she knew that the hourglass was somehow at the heart of it. It was no ordinary artifact; it was a gateway to the past.

Brimming with aromatic plants, exotic fruits, and beautiful carvings, the marketplace stalls in ancient Delphi were a riot of color and sound, forming a maze of sensory delights along the paved streets. Along with the faint tang of salt from the sea, the air was heavy with the aroma of incense. Despite the bustle of daily life, one stall attracted Mira's attention with its peculiar charm.

It was adorned with intricate sun motifs—golden medallions, brilliant amber gemstones, and small, intricate trinkets that seemed to shimmer and glow as if kissed by the light itself. A soft warmth radiated from the stall, a warmth that wasn't entirely of the sun, but something else, something ancient. Mira paused, her heart quickening as she studied the items laid out before her. Something about the stall felt familiar, as though it were calling to her.

Her colleagues were still captivated by the surrounding spectacle, but Mira felt an undeniable pull toward the elderly vendor sitting behind the counter. His age-worn face was lined with deep wrinkles, but his eyes—sharp and expressive—held an intensity that made her feel as if he could see straight through her. His lips curled into a knowing smile as he beckoned her closer.

"Ah, travelers from beyond the seas!" The vendor's voice was soft, yet carried a weight that felt like the echo of a thousand years. "Thou seemest lost, yet full of wonder. Hast thou come to seek Apollo's wisdom, or did the sun itself call thee here?"

Mira stepped forward, her pulse quickening as she locked eyes with him. The weight of the moment settled on her shoulders. The faint hum of the marketplace around her seemed to fade as if the world had momentarily paused.

"We're here to learn about Delphi and the Oracle," Mira said, her voice steady, though a part of her felt as though she were walking on the edge of something vast. "But we also wish to know of Helios... and his temple."

The vendor's smile deepened, as though he had been waiting for these very words. He leaned forward, his wrinkled hands resting on the counter. "Ah, the Temple of Helios… a place of which few speak, and fewer still shall look upon. It is no mere temple of stone or marble, but a vessel forged by the sun's very will. A thing of light and power, verily, but also of darkness, should it fall to unworthy hands."

"Helios..." Mira said, her voice barely a whisper. "He was not only a god of light. He created something, didn't he? Something powerful. The Prism."

The vendor's eyes seemed to deepen, his smile fading into something that resembled both caution and sorrow. "Aye, the Prism of Helios. A boon from the god unto the world, yet not one to be taken in lightness. Some call it a treasure; others, a curse. It is said to contain the very light of the sun within, a force so pure, so puissant, that it may bend time and space. They who seek it must reckon with more than they wot."

The vendor's gaze grew solemn, and the air around them seemed to be still. "To seek the Prism is to seek thy fate, and fate, my child, is a cruel mistress. She gives, but she takes. Thou must be ready to face what thou awakenest."

As Mira stood there, stunned by his words, the vendor, his face softening once more into a smile. "Ye seek the temple? Then seek it, if ye dare. But remember this: sometimes, the greatest power lies in the smallest of choices. And sometimes... the road ye walk is not the road ye think ye will follow."

With that, he leaned back, his gaze drifting to the horizon as if he were already seeing something far beyond the bustling market. His words hung in the air, heavy with meaning, like the first rays of dawn—dangerous yet irresistible.

"Well... that was intense," Josh said with a half-nervous laugh.

The further they approached the center of Delphi, the more excitement swept across the city. The Pythia Festival was nearing, and preparations were in full gear. Vendors' voices echoed like a harmonious chant as they sold little clay sculptures of the gods and beautiful wreaths. Intricate murals adorned the walls, painted by artisans using pigments so vivid they seemed to be alive. Musicians tuned their instruments in the open courtyards, while dancers practiced intricate movements.

Carrying pots of oil and aromatic herbs, a procession of priests and priestesses in flowing white robes marched solemnly toward the temple. The ritualistic perfection of their motions fascinated Mira, who stopped to observe them.

Suddenly, a young man approached them, his dark hair catching the sunlight, smiling warmly.

Nikos said to the group, “Welcome to Delphi, noble friends! Ye have come at a most fortuitous time. The Festival of the Pythia is nigh, and it shall be a spectacle most extraordinary!”

Mira, intrigued, glanced at her friends. “A festival? What does that involve?”

Nikos said in a secretive tone, “Ah, ’tis a grand celebration of prophecy and heavenly power. Music, dance, and a few surprising events will fill the city as the Oracle delivers visions. Wouldst ye care to join me? It is an experience not to be missed!”

“Will the Oracle appear for real?” Annie asked in a whispered voice, as though talking too loudly might upset the gods.

Nikos pointed to the audience and said, “’Tis not only about the Oracle. Yes, prophecy is celebrated at the festival, but so are life and community. ‘Tis a time when Delphi becomes more than just a city, but a gateway to the divine.”

Mira nodded, growing more enthusiastic. “I’d like to see it all. What else happens at the festival?”

Nikos’s eyes glowed, “Feasts that last until dawn, contests of wisdom and strength, music and dance, and ceremonies to honor the gods.”

With a gleam of excitement in his eyes, Joshua turned to face Mira, while Annie clutched her hands together, her face glowing with fascination.

Annie said. "We have to experience this together! It sounds like the adventure of a lifetime."

As they moved through the bustling marketplace, Nikos began to weave tales that painted vivid images in their minds.

Nikos continued with a spark of respect in his gaze. "The Oracle, dear friends, is held in utmost esteem within these hallowed lands. From distant realms, weary souls journey to seek her fabled counsel. There exists a tale of a pilgrim, steeped in despair, who received a prophecy that guided him to hidden treasure, transforming his fate forevermore."

Mira leaned in closer, captivated by his words as her imagination sparked to life.

Nikos lowered his voice to a hushed tone, his eyes gleaming with reverence. "Hearken unto me, for there exists a legend of sacred rites performed within the temple's embrace. The high priestess, resplendent in her beauty, doth dance beneath the soft light of the moon, invoking the gods to bestow their blessings upon the people. In such sacred moments, the veil that divideth our world from the divine groweth thin, revealing the wonders that lie beyond."

Jasper's eyes widened with wonder as he stepped closer. "I've read about those rituals! They're said to be incredibly powerful. We must try to document it!"

Mira nodded, caught up in the excitement like a child in Disneyland "Yes! I want to see it all!"

Tony leaned in, eyes sparkling. "Imagine the insights we could gain! This could revolutionize everything we know about ancient practices!"

As they continued through the market, Mira felt a sense of adventure welling up inside her.

"So, what kind of surprises should we expect at this festival?" Mira asked, her curiosity piqued.

Nikos laughed. "Oh, there shall be contests, labyrinths filled with riddles, and even a dance-off to appease the gods. If ye art brave enough, we could enter the trials together."

Mira's heart raced at the thought, and Joshua chimed in with enthusiasm.

Joshua said eagerly, "Count me in! I have always desired to test my skills against ancient challenges!"

Just then, an uproar flared up nearby. A group of townsfolk had gathered, their faces illuminated with excitement.

Nikos pulled them closer. "Come, let us see what fascinates the folks!"

As they approached, Mira saw a man dressed as a priest, his voice booming over the crowd.

Priest said, "Gather, gather! The Oracle hath spoken of a darkness looming over Delphi! A hero must arise to confront it!"

Mira turned to Nikos, her pulse quickening. "What does that mean? Are they truly expecting someone to save them?"

Nikos said, his expression turning serious, "'Tis more than mere tale. Legends hold power here. They believe in omens, and at times the bound betwixt myth and reality doth blur."

Mira felt a shiver run down her spine, an exhilarating fear. She couldn't shake the feeling that her presence here was no accident.

With a worried expression, Annie asks, "Do you think we could actually make a difference?"

Tony replied, "Why not? We have crossed time itself! We cannot stand idly by whilst the city needs aid!"

Nikos noticed their apprehension. "Whatever may come, we shall face it together. Ye are not alone."

The crowd erupted in cheers as the priest continued, promising great rewards for those who would undertake the quest. Mira exchanged a glance with Nikos, and in that moment, an unspoken agreement formed between them.

With hearts pounding and spirits high, Mira, Nikos, and her colleagues stepped into the unknown, ready to embrace whatever challenges lay ahead—be it mythical beasts, ancient riddles, or the truths that awaited them in the heart of Delphi.

As they made their way through the marketplace, the crowd thickened. Drums began to beat in the distance, a slow, hypnotic rhythm that drew people toward the central square. Mira and her team followed, curiosity pulling them like a tide.

As the day progressed, the team toured every corner of Delphi, each more captivating than the last. Tony cheered as they watched a wrestling competition, where contestants engaged in fierce combat, their muscles straining under the weight of effort and sweat. The crowd roared with excitement as each wrestler displayed feats of strength and agility, echoing the ancient spirit of athleticism. They marveled at the pottery booths, where artists skillfully shaped clay into magnificent sculptures of heroes and gods, their hands steady and confident as they worked. The vibrant colors and intricate designs left them in awe, connecting them to a world long gone yet somehow still present. As the sun sank low on the horizon, the city transformed. The streets were illuminated with lanterns and flaming torches, casting flickering shadows that danced across the stone. The scent of roasting meat and fresh bread filled the air, mingling with the faint smell of night-blooming flowers. As the air grew cooler, the festival's enthusiasm simply grew stronger. The sound of music—lutes, flutes, and the deep hum of drums—echoed through the city as laughter and song intertwined with the scent of the night. The ancient world was alive with color, sound, and celebration, and the team felt as though they had stepped into something timeless.

Nikos gestured them to follow him, saying, "Come. The moonlit dance beginneth soon, and ye must not miss it."

The team followed him, climbing a narrow path that led up the hillside. As they reached the open-air area, they were greeted by the sight of stone benches filled with spectators. The air was crisp, carrying a faint scent of pine and salt from the distant sea breeze. The view was breathtaking: the vast expanse of water glittered in the distance, its surface kissed by the fading light of the sunset, while above them, the first stars began to blink into existence, one by one, like scattered diamonds in the darkening sky.

The stage was set beneath the canopy of ancient olive trees, their gnarled branches swaying gently in the evening breeze. The dancers were dressed in robes of pure white, each one adorned with golden threads that shimmered with every movement. Their feet barely seemed to touch the ground as they moved in perfect harmony, their bodies flowing like water. In the center of the stage stood a mesmerizing beauty draped in a golden robe, encrusted with tiny, twinkling crystals, catching the soft glow of the moon. The light from the moon caught on the crystals, making them glitter like stardust. Her dark, curly hair, braided with sparkling jewels, framed her face like a halo, and her eyes, a deep, mysterious shade of violet, held an almost otherworldly allure. Every gaze in the audience was locked on her, drawn by the quiet intensity she exuded. As the rhythmic beat of the drums began to pulse through the air, the dancers moved together, their feet and bodies weaving a story of grace and power that seemed to transcend time itself. The music filled the space, pulling everyone into the spell of the dance.

The dance was unlike anything Mira had ever seen. It was graceful yet powerful, each movement precise and purposeful, as if every gesture told a story, each expression of the body rooted in the weight of ancient tradition. The lead dancer, radiant in her golden robe, seemed to glow in the moonlight, her figure a blend of human and divine. With each turn and lift of her arms, she transformed—no longer merely a performer, but a living symbol of the ancient world's sacred mysteries. Mira watched in awe, feeling as if the dance had unlocked something deep within her, some ancient echo resonating through her bones.

The night ended with a feast, the likes of which Mira could hardly believe. Tables groaned under the weight of roasted meats, fresh bread, and fruits so ripe they seemed to burst with flavor. Wine flowed freely, and the sound of laughter filled the air.

As Mira sat with her friends, her thoughts drifted back to the vendor's words and the tale of the Prism. She knew this was just the beginning. The Festival of the Pythia had awakened something in her—a determination to uncover the mysteries of Helios and the power that lay hidden within his temple.

And as the stars shone brightly overhead, Mira made a silent vow: whatever challenges lay ahead, she would face them. Delphi had become more than a destination. It was her destiny.

✦ ✦ ✦

Chapter Four

Whispers of the Oracle

The buzzing of cicadas filled the cool night air as Mira and her companions followed Nikos to his family home. The glow of the moonlit dance still lingered in their minds, an enchanting spectacle that had filled their hearts with awe. Nikos led them through narrow, curving paths edged with olive trees. The leaves rustled gently in the breeze, whispering secrets of the old world. Crickets chirped in the distance, and the rich scent of night jasmine hung heavy in the air, mingling with hints of thyme and earth.

The path sloped gently upward, offering glimpses of the valley below—a sweeping landscape that stretched endlessly, the hills bathed in the soft light of the stars. Lanterns placed along the trail flickered softly, lighting their way with a golden hue. As they walked, Mira noticed ancient pottery fragments embedded in the path and the occasional carved stone partially hidden by overgrown vines—remnants of a long-forgotten past.

They arrived at a small stone house nestled on the hillside, its walls aged and weathered but sturdy, bearing the character of generations. Creeping ivy climbed one side of the building, and a small terracotta roof overhung the entrance. A faint glow came from inside, the light of oil lamps casting a welcoming warmth through the open windows. Laughter and the soft clatter of dishes drifted out, blending with the nocturnal sounds.

"Welcome home," Nikos said, slowly pushing open the wooden door. Inside, the air was filled with the scent of freshly baked bread and herbs drying in bundles near the hearth. A woman, her hair streaked with silver but her face radiant with kindness, approached them with a warm smile and curious eyes, speaking in gentle tones that carried the lilt of an ancient dialect.

"Ye be travelers, new to this place, aye?" she said, her voice soft. She introduced herself, "Me, Nikos mama, Callisto."

Nikos' father, Timotheos—a lean man with bluish-gray eyes that held a depth speaking of wisdom, patience, and a lifetime of stories— greeted them with a kind smile and outstretched his wrinkled hands. His skin was sun-worn and calloused, the hands of someone who had worked the land with quiet dignity for decades. He ushered them in with a calm presence that instantly made Mira feel at ease. Moments later, Eleni, Nikos' younger sister, peeked out shyly from behind her mother, her beautiful sparkling gray eyes flickering with curiosity. A small smile tugged at the corners of her lips when she saw Mira.

"It's lovely," Mira said in a soft voice, admiring the room's simplicity: a loom in the corner where Eleni had likely been working, a stack of clay pots beside it, and a solid wooden table with a woven cloth bearing intricate patterns of olive branches and laurel leaves. The home was modest but deeply comforting. Its walls held laughter, toil, and tradition – a loving, hard-working home. Mira felt the weight of their journey ease slightly, replaced by the warmth of human kindness.

After enjoying a humble, satisfying dinner of bread, olives, and cheese served with clay mugs of cool water, everyone settled for the night. Mira, Annie, and Eleni curled up on a woven mat close to the hearth. Lying on the open porch, Tony, Josh, Jasper, and Nikos took in the splendor of the night sky, its stars shining brightly overhead. As Timotheos moved through the house, gently putting out the lamps one by one, he hummed an old lullaby—low and steady, like the rhythm of the earth itself. The sound seemed to wrap around Mira like a blanket, soothing and familiar, lulling her into a state of peace that she hadn't experienced in weeks.

Next Day

They awoke the next morning to the aroma of freshly baked bread. After a home-cooked authentic Greek breakfast, they waved farewell to Nikos's family, receiving their blessings and warm smiles as they headed out for Apollo's temple. Together, Nikos and Mira settled into a comfortable pace as they climbed the rugged path that led to the cliffs. The morning sun flooded the landscape with golden light, and the air was thick with the aroma of pine and wildflowers. Birds flitted from branch to branch, their morning songs weaving into the peaceful silence between Mira and Nikos. The rhythmic crunch of their footsteps on the gravel path mingled with the rustling of the wind through the trees.

"There is something I must speak, Mira," Nikos said thoughtfully.

She looked at him curiously. "What is it?"

Nikos said with his eyes fixed on the horizon, his expression distant. "For years, I have dreamt of travelers from afar. In mine dreams, they came to Delphi seeking the wisdom of the Oracle. I knew not their faces, nor their purpose, but I felt their presence."

"Mayhap," Nikos replied with a faint smile. "I knew not who they were at the time, only that they bore the burden of fate upon their shoulders. When I met ye, I felt mine dreams had come alive."

Mira felt an icy chill run down her spine, but it wasn't fear; it was a bizarre, exciting recognition of fate's intertwined threads. She asked, "Do you think the Oracle knew we were coming?"

Nikos nodded solemnly. "The Oracle knows much, though she speaks only what thou art ready to hear. What brought thee here, Mira, know that thy purpose is greater than thou canst yet comprehend."

The weight of his words hung over Mira like a blanket as they walked in silence for a while. Looking back at her squad, she saw them giggling at something Jasper had said. Although their friendship served as her compass, she was also overwhelmed with wonder and fear at the realization that their journey was a part of something greater.

"Have you ever spoken with the Oracle yourself?" Mira asked.

Nikos hesitated, then gave a slow nod. "Once. When I was a boy. She spoke in riddles I did not understand back then. But now, looking at thee, at thy friends, I think... perhaps she was not speaking to the child I was, but to the moment I would help guide."

Long shadows stretched across the rocky cliffs as the morning sun rose higher in the sky. As they made their way up toward the temple, their footsteps echoed along the narrow route. A shepherd waved to them from a nearby field, his flock grazing quietly on the dew-covered grass. The scent of crushed earth lingered with every step, grounding Mira in the reality of where she stood. With his spear in hand and accustomed ease, Nikos led the way, inspecting the terrain.

Annie gave an exaggerated sigh, her face turning red from the effort. "Are we there yet? This looks like an infinite path."

Jasper laughed, wiping the sweat off his brow. "You've escaped lethal traps and outwitted ancient puzzles, but a little hilly climb is your worst enemy?"

"This isn't comparable!" Annie responded, giving him a mock look. "Just rocks, rocks, and more rocks—no adrenaline rush to distract me."

With a smile, Tony said, "Consider it training. This will prepare you to run a marathon."

Mira, who was walking behind Nikos, giggled at the jokes but maintained her attention on their surroundings. The air grew cooler as they climbed higher, and the rustle of leaves seemed to carry whispers along the breeze.

Nikos said softly, "There is a silence here. The closer we draw nigh, the more the world doth seem to hearken."

Josh, who was at the back, looked nervously over his shoulder. "Or it could simply be the peace before the storm hits. There's often something ready to leap out at you in these ancient places."

"Thy prudence is not untrue," Nikos said, his tone serious. "Though the holy place is sacred, it is also guarded. Legends speak of the creatures that test the worth of those who seek the Oracle's wisdom."

Mira felt a chill run down her spine. "What kind of creatures?"

Nikos shook his head. "Nobody alive today hath seen them. Only the Oracle knows of what awaits ahead, and she sets forth her trials to each seeker in a way that is special to their journey."

The group went silent as his comments weighed heavily on them. A breathtaking view of the valley below stood out when they turned a bend in the route. Streams sparkled, and patches of forest dotted the landscape, with green hills that stretched to the horizon.

Mira paused to absorb it all and whispered, "It's beautiful."

They continued along the winding path, which soon began to descend sharply. The terrain became increasingly difficult and steep as they moved lower. The sound of flowing water reached their ears, and they shortly noticed a narrow stream running across their path. A wooden bridge spanned the gap, its planks worn but strong.

Nikos cautioned, "Careful," as he crossed the bridge. "It's old wood. One by one only."

The murmur of the water below served as a continual reminder of the drop beneath them as they crossed one by one. Arriving at the other side, Annie exhaled with relief.

Nikos gestured for them to follow him, saying, "Just a little farther now."

The path began to rise steadily, leading them uphill. The forest started to thin out as they climbed up, with the tall trees giving way to rocky outcroppings and smaller shrubs. The air became cooler, and a faint aroma of incense wafted toward them.

When they stepped out onto a plateau, the temple was visible. With its marble columns shining in the sunlight, the ancient structure stood out sharply against the rocky surroundings. The edges were worn over time, but its grandeur had not faded.

Tony's voice was hardly audible above a whisper when he said, "Wow. It's amazing."

Mira's breath froze in her chest as she gazed at the temple's overwhelming presence, which was both captivating and challenging. This was it—the point where secrets would be revealed and their journey would evolve into a path; they weren't sure about.

✦ ✦ ✦

A Sacred Encounter

Warm light filtered through the temple's high windows as the sun sank low in the sky, casting golden shafts across the ancient stone floor. Mira's pulse was racing with a mixture of nerves and excitement as she stood within the marble embrace of the sacred space. Behind her, the plateau outside was quiet, the forest below now a distant memory after the long ascent. Nikos was beside her, adjusting his tunic, his face a blend of pride and concern.

"Art thou prepared?" Nikos asked, his voice steady despite the weight of the moment.

Mira took a deep breath, grounding herself in the present moment. "I am," she replied, trying to quell the fluttering in her stomach. She glanced at her team, who were exchanging excited glances. The air was thick with anticipation as they prepared for the challenges ahead.

"Remember," Nikos continued, his expression serious, "the Oracle's words bear great weight. We must needs approach this quest with courage and wisdom."

Mira nodded, taking in the gravity of his words. They had entered a world where legends breathed through stone and shadow, and every decision could alter the course of fate.

The atmosphere inside the temple was dense with incense and devotion, steeped in history and mystery. The columns rose magnificently, guarding the entryway like sentinels from the past. A faint breeze stirred through the open archways, whispering ancient secrets across the stone.

In the faint light, the altar was decked with offerings such as laurel wreaths, silver coins, and tiny figurines. Each offering spoke of devotion and hope, a tribute to the seekers who had come before her.

"Here dost thou wait, as seekers have done before thee," Nikos said, leading her to a circle of worn stones. "Prepare thyself for the Oracle's words, for they come veiled in riddles."

"What should I ask?" Mira's voice trembled slightly, excitement and apprehension intertwining within her.

"Ask that which thou truly seekest," he replied, placing a reassuring hand over hers. "But prepare thyself, for the truth is not always gentle."

Mira closed her eyes and felt a wave of energy fill the room, aural power calling her to listen. The sounds of the temple faded away, leaving behind a sweet, melodious voice that resonated in her consciousness.

"Τί ἐστίν, ὦ τέκνον τοῦ μέλλοντος, ὃ ζητεῖς;" ("What is it that you seek, O child of the future?")

Startled, Mira opened her eyes. The air shimmered, and she sensed the presence of something deeper than herself.

"I seek guidance... about my journey, my purpose here," she said softly, her pulse hammering in her chest.

"Γνῶθι τοῦτο: ὁ ἀναβαίνων δρόμος οὐκ ἐστὶ μόνον σός. Οἱ ἱκανόντες τῆς μοῖρας ἀλληλοδιεξάγονται. Πίστις τῷ δρόμῳ, ὅτι ἐν τοῖς σκότοις ἡ ἰσχὺς σου κεῖται."

("Know this: The path you walk is not solely for yourself. The threads of fate intertwine. Trust in the journey, for in the shadows lies your strength.")

As the words faded, Mira felt a wave of clarity wash over her. She turned to Nikos, who was watching her intently, a knowing smile on his face.

"What dost thou hear?" he asked, his curiosity evident.

"I must embrace the journey, to trust in the path ahead. It is about more than just me," she replied, her voice growing stronger.

Nikos nodded; his expression serious. "Words of wisdom from the Oracle. Much lies ahead, and thou shalt need strength and courage."

With newfound determination, they left the temple. Rather than retracing their steps, Nikos led them down a lesser-known path through the sacred grove, said to guard hidden truths and ancient trials. The sun was now setting behind the mountains, painting the sky in hues of orange and purple. As they descended the cliffs, Mira felt a renewed sense of purpose, ready to face whatever challenges lay ahead.

But as they stepped back into the grove, the air shimmered again, swirling with a faint mist that whispered secrets of the trials to come. The voice of the Oracle lingered in her mind, a reminder of the intertwining destinies they were yet to explore.

"Prepare thy minds and hearts," Nikos continued, "for the trials draw nigh. Only by proving thy worth shall the path forward be revealed."

Mira felt the weight of destiny pressing against her, but this time, she welcomed it. With Nikos and her friends by her side, she was ready to embrace whatever lay ahead, guided by the whispers of the Oracle, the words of the vendor, and the strength of their shared journey.

Annie's voice, a mix of excitement and fear, broke the eerie silence. "Do you think we're really going to face something dangerous?" she whispered, her eyes darting around the misty grove.

Tony, ever the optimist, gave her a reassuring smile. "Whatever it is, we'll face it together," he said, his voice steady.

Mira felt a surge of gratitude for her team. Their unity was her strength. "We're stronger together," she affirmed, her voice firm. "Let's be brave."

As they moved farther into the forest, the air became heavier, charged with unseen energy. They were surrounded by fog that clouded their view, creating an unearthly environment. The trees, ancient and gnarled, seemed to lean inward, their twisted branches forming ghostly silhouettes through the swirling mist. Their senses were teased by the dancing shadows at the edge of their vision. The swirling mist thickened. Then, without warning, the ground began to rumble beneath them. The tremor was subtle at first, like a warning heartbeat deep within the earth, but it grew more pronounced, more insistent. They were chilled by an eerie, deep roar that echoed through the trees – a sound that didn't just touch the ears but rattled the spine.

"What was that?" Josh muttered, his voice barely above a whisper, his confidence slipping as his gaze darted about.

Nikos raised his hand to silence the group. "Listen," he said, his brows furrowed with concentration.

With the sound of branches snapping, the growl became more intense. Mira's heart raced. Every thump inside her chest felt like a drumbeat of impending danger. The legends described dangerous guardians protecting the Oracle's sanctuary, beasts that would put those seeking its wisdom to the test. Despite her growing worry, Mira's voice remained steady as she said, "We need to be ready. Let's devise a strategy."

Ever the strategist, Jasper proposed, "What if we split up? Distract it from the center of the grove?"

"Nay," Nikos interjected firmly. "We remain together. Our unity is that which grants us strength. We shall face whatever waits in the shadows— as one."

As the creature approached, the mist cleared, revealing an unspeakable sight: a Pyracmon, straight out of mythology. A monstrous form, eight feet tall and brimming with raw power, was a terrifying blend of man and beast. Its bluish-green skin, thick and leathery, covered a powerfully built, almost ape-like body. It stood on three huge, clawed toes, its long arms ending in equally menacing claws, ready to strike. The head—a lion's face framed by a thick, bristling mane, was crowned with two sharp horns. But it was the eyes—the twin orbs burning with an eerie golden light, holding the cold, ancient hunger of a predator that held the true horror: Pyracmon, a predator of mythic proportions.

"Get ready!" Nikos exclaimed, stepping forward as the beast let out a deafening roar.

Despite her racing heart, Mira felt a wave of insight. The Oracle's words lingered in her mind: "In the shadows lies thy strength." Her voice was firm as she said, "We'll face this together. On my count, we attack!"

However, their attempt to gather was abruptly interrupted by a deep, guttural groan from the earth beneath them. Jagged fissures snaked across the forest floor, yawning open like hungry maws, revealing dark, unseen depths that threatened to swallow them whole.

"Everyone, back!" Mira screamed, pulling herself to the side, barely missing the crumbling ground.

"Now we're fighting against the earth too!" Jasper exclaimed, a hint of panic in his voice.

"We need to move!" Mira shouted. As they crossed the treacherous terrain, the Pyracmon attacked, striking Josh with its long, powerful arm and knocking him off balance.

"No!" Mira screamed reaching for him.

Tony caught Josh's arm and pulled him back just in time as he stumbled. "Stay together!" he urged.

With a roar, the Pyracmon unleashed a burst of fire, igniting the dry brush from its lion-like mouth. The group scattered as flames surged toward them.

"Watch the fire!" Annie screamed, running for shelter behind a massive boulder. Relentless, the beast swung its tail, toppling obstacles and spreading mayhem.

"Use the boulders!" Mira called out pointing toward the solid rocks. "We can shield ourselves and create opportunities to strike!" Despite the turmoil, they began to strategize. Mira spotted an opening as the beast unleashed its fiery breath once more. "Now! Aim for its flanks!"

With precision, the group attacked, darting from boulder to boulder, coordinating their moves. However, the Pyracmon cleverly retaliated, feigning withdrawal and luring them in before unleashing a powerful whirlwind that knocked them back. Tony's heart pounded. "We must not allow it to control the fight!" Even amidst the disorienting chaos, his gaze locked onto something glinting at the center of the creature's chest – a large, multifaceted jewel embedded just above its heart. "That's its core! Go for the gem!" he shouted.

They scrambled to reposition, huddling behind a cluster of boulders, forming a makeshift wall of defense against the Pyracmon's relentless advance. The beast pounced again, and Nikos shouted, "Now!" Together, they surged forward, but with surprising agility for its size, the beast twisted just in time, its thrashing tail knocking Jasper off his feet.

"Jasper!" Annie cried out, her voice laced with terror. But in the brief moment of confusion, Nikos saw his chance. With a daring leap, fueled by adrenaline and desperation, he plunged his spear deep into the glowing jewel. A violent shockwave rippled through the woodland, the air crackling with energy as the gem shattered with a deafening explosion. With a final, thunderous roar that echoed through the now silent trees, the Pyracmon's colossal body trembled violently before collapsing to the earth with a ground-shaking thud, finally vanquished.

Panting heavily, their bodies aching and bruised, Mira turned to her team. Their faces, streaked with dirt and sweat, were a mixture of disbelief and profound relief. A shaky smile touched her lips. "We did it," she whispered, struggling to catch her breath, the weight of the impossible victory settling upon them.

Nikos rushed to Jasper's side, followed by everyone else. "Jasper!" he shouted, shaking him gently. There was no response. Panic gripped Mira as she knelt beside him. "Give some water," he said urgently. Josh quickly pulled out his water bottle from his bag and splashed it gently on Jasper's face.

With a start, Jasper's eyes fluttered open. "What happened?" he murmured, confusion clouding his gaze.

"You took a hit," Tony said, his voice filled with concern. "Can you get up?"

When Nikos saw the water bottle, he looked puzzled. It was something he had never seen before. "What is this?" he inquired. Josh gave Nikos a blank stare. Mira abruptly interrupted, "It's not safe here. We need to move quickly."

Jasper struggled to rise, but a sharp pain shot through his side, forcing him to gasp. "I can't move," he panted, his face pale.

"Don't worry. We've got you," Josh said, kneeling beside him. He and Tony helped Jasper to his feet, supporting him as they started to walk.

"We'll get you back to safety," Mira reassured him, her heart heavy with concern for her friend.

"How many challenges are we to face yet!" gasped Annie, as they made their way through the grove, the echoes of their battle fading behind them.

Jasper was heavily reliant on Josh and Tony as they staggered through the grove after the encounter with the Pyracmon. As she looked at his pale face, Mira's heart ached, but she was stronger than ever.

Despite the chaos they had just experienced, the young warrior, Nikos, stepped steadily, his face tired but determined.

"I see now why the Oracle called thee and thy friends," Nikos remarked quietly.

Mira stared at him, her tired eyes flickering with curiosity. "Why is that?"

"Because ye are the travelers of my dream," Nikos said simply. "Your strength lieth not in your weapons, nor in your knowledge, but in your unity. Together, ye shall win trials that break others."

His words resonated deeply with Mira, echoing the Oracle's riddle: The threads of fate intertwine.

After a little silence, she murmured, "Nikos, I believe you are also a part of this destiny. The Oracle did not simply bring us here; she brought us to you."

Nikos smiled, his expression both humble and proud. "Then let us walk this path together, whitherso'er it may lead."

As the mist of the grove began to clear, revealing the path back to the village, Mira felt a flicker of hope despite the challenges ahead. They were stronger together, and with the wisdom of the Oracle and the steadfastness of Nikos by their side, they would face whatever awaited them.

✦ ✦ ✦

Chapter Five

The Ripple Effect

In the Present Day, at a nearby site

"Dr. Reed!" A young assistant's voice cracked through the dry heat, carrying an edge of urgency.

She looked up, squinting through the glare. "What is it, Iris?"

"I think you need to see this."

Moments later, Reed stood over a newly unearthed object. It wasn't pottery or stone—this was something else entirely. Carefully, she took the object in her gloved hands, wiping away the dirt. Her breath caught.

It was a beautiful bottle. A perfectly intact, elegant glass water bottle, its surface etched with faint patterns that looked impossibly modern.

"Is this... contamination?" Iris asked, glancing nervously at the artifact.

Reed shook her head, her trained eye noting the distinct signs of age—weathered edges and the slight iridescence of glass buried for millennia. But the craftsmanship was undeniably contemporary.

"Run a preliminary dating test," she said, her voice steady despite the unease growing in her chest.

The results came a few days later.

Dr. Reed reviewed the initial test results on her laptop, her brows knitting in confusion.

"Confirmed sediment layering suggests it's been buried for at least... 3,000 years," she murmured, almost to herself. She glanced up, meeting Iris's wide-eyed gaze. "But that's impossible."

Iris glanced at the bottle in her hands, still carefully inspecting it. "It's not just the age that's strange," she said. "Look at this."

She pointed to the base of the bottle, where faint, almost illegible markings could be seen beneath the grime. Reed leaned closer, her breath catching as the symbols became clearer—letters, arranged in a way that seemed... familiar.

"Is that… English?" Reed asked, her voice low.

Iris carefully cleaned the surface with a delicate brush, revealing more of the text. Though faded, it was unmistakable: a brand logo, a design that looked eerily modern. The words "Hydra-Pure", engraved, stood out in the light.

Reed's hands tightened around the edge of the table. "This brand came to market... what, ten to twelve years ago?"

Iris looked up from the bottle, her expression unreadable. "It can't be," she whispered. "But how is that even possible?"

Dr. Reed pressed her fingers to her temple, trying to make sense of it.

"We need to run more tests," Reed said, her voice firm despite the storm brewing in her mind. "Isotopic analysis, anything we can get."

Iris nodded, but the hesitation in her eyes betrayed her. "You don't think... I mean, how likely is it that something from our time period ended up in the past?"

Reed didn't answer immediately. Instead, she studied the bottle, running her fingers over the smooth glass. For a moment, the weight of their discovery settled over her like a physical force. There had been rumors about time anomalies; strange artifacts and unexplained occurrences—but she never imagined she'd be involved in one.

"I don't know," she finally said. "But we need to find out."

They set to work in silence, Iris handling the bottle carefully as Reed prepared the necessary equipment. Days passed; each test result was more perplexing than the last. The sediment layers, the age of the bottle—it all aligned with ancient timelines. Yet, the brand clearly belonged to a modern company, with a manufacturing date that should have placed it no earlier than twelve years ago.

"It doesn't add up," Iris muttered, rechecking the readings for the nth time.

Reed looked up, her mind racing. If something or someone had altered history, what else had changed in ways they couldn't yet comprehend? The implications were terrifying.

"We might be looking at something much bigger than an artifact," Reed said quietly, her gaze drifting back to the bottle.

✦ ✦ ✦

Mira and her Team in the Past

Back in the distant past, Mira and her team continued their search for the Helios Prism, unaware of the far-reaching effects their actions were triggering.

"Hey Josh! Pass me your bottle," Jasper called out

"Sure," Josh replied, frowning as he rummaged through his bag.

"I guess I left it back in the woods."

Meanwhile, the small water bottle with its name *Hydra-Pure* engraved on it—one that had unknowingly traveled through time, lay hidden in the earth, its modern design buried beneath millennia of soil.

✦ ✦ ✦

Present Day – Investigation Deepens

Reed and Iris sat in the lab, reviewing the results from the dating analysis. The machine had run tests overnight, and now the data glowed on the screen in front of them.

Reed's eyes scanned the report carefully. "Alright, let's break this down. The outer sediment layers confirm burial for approximately 3,000 years, which matches the surrounding soil samples."

Iris nodded, taking notes. "But the composition of the glass... it doesn't add up. The formula suggests a level of refinement that wasn't possible until recent decades—high-purity silica and trace elements consistent with modern production methods."

Reed tapped her fingers on the table thoughtfully. "So, the soil dates back thousands of years, but the bottle itself shouldn't exist in this context."

"There's more," Iris continued. "I examined the etching on the surface. Under magnification, the precision is too advanced for anything from ancient times—these markings were made using modern industrial techniques."

She paused, her voice tightening. "And then there's the branding—*Hydra-Pure*. As you said, that company wasn't even founded until twelve years ago."

Reed exhaled slowly, staring at the bottle resting inside its protective case across the room. "This isn't contamination. It's not a mistake. This bottle was used in our time and somehow ended up buried under layers of undisturbed earth that date back to the Bronze Age."

Iris swallowed hard. "But how?"

Reed didn't answer right away. Her mind was already racing through the implications, the possibilities, and what this discovery might mean for their understanding of history.

"We'll need to cross-verify everything," she finally said. "If these findings hold, we may be looking at evidence that time... might not be as linear as we thought."

Iris hesitated. "If we publish this, it could change everything."

Reed leaned back, her gaze fixed on the bottle. "Let's first make sure we know what we're dealing with."

Iris's phone buzzed sharply on the table, the vibration rattling against the hard surface. She barely glanced at the screen before answering.

"Mom?" she said, her voice puzzled at first. But the moment she heard her mother's frantic tone, her stomach tightened.

"Iris! Thank God! Are you okay?", her mom checked.

"Yeah, I'm fine. What's wrong?", Iris replied.

Her mom continued, "There's been an earthquake, a big one! I saw it on the news. They said it hit near Delphi. You've been working there, haven't you? I've been trying to reach you!"

Iris blinked, processing the words. She hadn't been in Delphi today. She and Dr. Reed had returned to the lab to analyze their findings. But her mother was not aware of that.

"Mom, I'm okay. We are not in Delphi today." She softened her tone, trying to ease the panic. "I promise, I'm safe."

Her mother exhaled shakily. "You scared me half to death. Just… please be careful, okay?"

"I will. I'll call you later," Iris said, just before disconnecting the call.

As soon as she ended the call, she turned to Dr. Reed, who had been watching her with mild concern.

"What was that about?" Reed asked.

"There's been an earthquake," Iris said, already reaching for her laptop. "Near Delphi."

Reed's eyebrows lifted slightly. "How bad?"

"Let's check."

Iris pulled up a news channel on YouTube and clicked on the first live report. The screen loaded to a breaking news broadcast, the red ticker at the bottom flashing: **EARTHQUAKE STRIKES GREECE – MAJOR TREMORS NEAR DELPHI AND ARACHOVA. POSSIBLE DAMAGE REPORTED.**

Iris and Reed leaned in as the footage switched to aerial shots, showing collapsed buildings, cracked roads, and dust clouds still settling over the affected regions. Delphi, in particular, had taken a heavy hit—ancient stone structures had crumbled, landslides had reshaped the landscape, and emergency responders were already on the ground.

Then, the broadcast cut to a new segment.

"We're now receiving exclusive drone footage from a newly exposed site near Delphi," the news anchor announced, her voice carrying a mix of urgency and intrigue. "Reports indicate that this area was previously uncharted—until now."

The screen shifted to a bird's-eye view of the rugged terrain, where the earthquake had caused a massive section of the hillside to collapse. But that wasn't what caught Iris's attention.

"Wait… what is that?" she murmured.

Reed leaned forward, narrowing her eyes. Beneath the disturbed earth, partially unearthed by the quake, was what looked like a vast underground chamber.

The drone zoomed in, and the news anchor continued. "Scientists and paleontologists are being called to the site once it is deemed safe to visit, as there is growing speculation that this could be evidence that dinosaurs once roamed Greece."

The footage zoomed in further, capturing the exposed bones with greater clarity. The skeletal structure, still partially buried under layers of earth and rock, was immense. Ribs curved like the hull of an ancient ship, and vertebrae stretched in a long, twisting formation.

"Although Greece has never been considered a site for dinosaur fossils due to its prehistoric geography, experts are now questioning whether new evidence could challenge that assumption," the news anchor continued. "If confirmed, this discovery could rewrite what we know about prehistoric life in the region."

Iris exhaled slowly. "A dinosaur fossil?" she muttered. "That would be huge."

Reed, however, didn't look convinced. She was studying the screen with a deep frown, her fingers tapping absently against the table.

"Something's off," she murmured. "Look at the structure of those bones. If that's a dinosaur, it's unlike any species I've ever known."

Iris had a sense of unease creeping through her. She wanted to believe the news report— that this was a groundbreaking paleontological discovery, a rare anomaly in Greece's geological history. But deep down, something didn't sit right.

And if her instincts were correct, the truth behind those bones was going to be far stranger than anyone could have imagined.

✦ ✦ ✦

Scientific and Media Frenzy

Reed leaned back in her chair, eyes fixed on the screen as the broadcast continued. Experts debated the fossil discovery, some cautiously optimistic, others outright dismissing the idea that anything significant had been found.

"The rock layers exposed by the earthquake are still being analyzed," one geologist explained. "While we can confirm that fossilized remains are present, we cannot yet determine their age or species."

Another panelist, a paleontologist, chimed in. "Greece is not known for dinosaur fossils, but that doesn't mean none exist. This could be an extraordinary find, or it could be something entirely different. We need more data before jumping to conclusions."

Reed exhaled slowly, rubbing her temple. "They're dancing around the facts," she muttered.

Iris glanced at her. "What do you mean?"

"They're hesitating. If this were an ordinary fossil discovery, they'd be more confident in their statements. Instead, they're being overly cautious; either because they don't have enough information or because something isn't adding up."

Iris nodded, her mind racing. "So, what now? Do we wait for more reports?"

Reed shook her head. "No. I know someone who might have some insight." She reached for her phone and scrolled through her contacts.

"Who?" asked Iris.

Reed continued, "Professor Alexander Savas. He was my mentor. If anyone understands the geological history of Greece and what could be buried beneath it, then, it's him."

Iris leaned forward. "Do you think he'll know anything about this?"

"There's only one way to find out."

Reed pressed the call button and lifted the phone to her ear, listening as the line rang.

✦ ✦ ✦

Chapter Six

A Call for Answers

Reed sat at her desk, rolling her pen between her fingers as she listened to the dial tone. She had hesitated before making the call, but the moment her old professor's voice came through the line, she knew she'd made the right choice.

"Reed." A voice came from the other end of the phone.

His voice hadn't changed. Still steady, still calm, still carrying that weight of experience that made her feel like a student again.

"Professor Savas," she said, leaning forward in her chair. "I hope I'm not catching you at a bad time."

A dry chuckle. "Retirement doesn't come with many obligations. But I have a feeling this isn't just a social call."

Iris sat nearby, scrolling through news reports, but her attention was on the conversation.

Reed glanced at Iris before responding. "The earthquake near Delphi. Have you seen the reports?"

Professor Savas replied, "Of course. Hard to miss. Quite the mess. What about it?"

She sighed, pinching the bridge of her nose. "I don't know yet. The site isn't supposed to contain dinosaur fossils, but there's something there. Something big. The layers of sediment they're pulling it from don't make sense."

More silence. A faint rustling paper? A book? She knew that sound well from the years spent in his office, where every answer seemed to be hidden between old pages.

"Professor?" she prompted.

Savas made a thoughtful noise. "And now there's a fossil where there shouldn't be one."

"Exactly," Reed said. "The reports are vague, but if the sediment is as old as they're saying, it shouldn't be yielding dinosaur fossils. Greece wasn't exactly a hotspot for them."

Savas hummed in agreement. "The landmass was mostly underwater back then. Any terrestrial fossils would be an anomaly."

"That's what's bothering me," Reed admitted. "I know the media loves to jump ahead, but if there really is something unusual there, I want to understand it before speculation takes over. And I figured if anyone could help me make sense of this, it's you."

A brief pause. Then, the sound of shuffling; she pictured him in his study, probably pulling a book from one of the towering shelves. "You always did ask the right questions," Savas said, a note of amusement in his voice. "And you're right to be skeptical. But, why this one?"

"I was there a few days before the quake. And…," Before Reed could finish, Professor Savas interrupted, "Tell me—this artifact you found, what exactly was it?"

Reed's gaze flicked to the protective case on the table, where the glass bottle rested. "A modern water bottle. Branded. Nothing ancient about it."

Silence. Then, a low chuckle. "Reed, I may be retired, but even I know you don't call an old professor just to talk about misplaced litter."

She smirked despite herself. "No. We carbon-dated the surrounding sediment. Three thousand years old. And yet, the bottle was buried beneath it."

Savas didn't answer right away. When he did, his voice had changed—lower, more serious. "And now, an earthquake unearths a fossil from a time that shouldn't exist here."

Reed exhaled, rubbing her temple. "It's not just one strange find; it's two, within days of each other. I don't believe in coincidences, but I don't have another explanation."

Savas was quiet for a moment, the faint sound of papers rustling on his end. She could almost picture him flipping through one of his old research notes, piecing together possibilities. "This doesn't add up," he finally said. "If the fossil is genuine, we're looking at something that challenges what we know about this region's prehistoric past. And if your artifact's dating holds, then…" He trailed off.

"Then something is interfering with history," Reed finished for him.

Savas let out a thoughtful sigh. "I'd like to say there's a logical answer, but these anomalies—you need to be careful how you present them. The scientific community won't entertain theories that suggest anything outside the natural order."

Reed leaned back, glancing at Iris, who was still deep in the news reports. "I know. That's why I want to get ahead of this before it spirals. I need real answers, not media speculation."

Savas was quiet for a moment before he spoke again, his tone thoughtful. "Reed, this isn't the kind of thing we can piece together over the phone."

He continued, "My home, tomorrow noon. And Reed?"

"Yes?" she asked, a beat of hesitation in her voice.

"Come with an open mind," the professor said, just before the line went dead.

Reed slowly set the phone down, staring at the laptop screen for a moment before looking up at Iris.

"That was… vague," Iris said, frowning.

Reed huffed a small laugh and shook her head. "That was classic, Professor Savas."

Iris tilted her head. "Think he knows something?"

Reed leaned back in her chair, crossing her arms. "He always does. The question is—how much is he willing to tell us?"

✦ ✦ ✦

Next Day

The hum of the car engine filled the silence as Reed navigated the road, her fingers tapping lightly against the steering wheel. Iris sat beside her, eyes fixed on the passing scenery. The morning air was crisp, the sky clear; a stark contrast to the chaos unfolding just hours away in Delphi.

Iris reached for the radio dial, twisting it until a news channel crackled through the speakers.

"—as the aftermath of the Delphi earthquake continues to unfold, experts are calling for more analysis before jumping to conclusions. However, rumors are already swirling about the unusual fossil discovered, with some suggesting it could rewrite history," reported a local anchor.

A different voice took over, this one brisk and authoritative. "We have no verified information yet. Until thorough analysis is conducted, any speculation about what this means—whether geological anomaly or groundbreaking discovery—is premature."

Reed sighed and shook her head. "At least someone's trying to keep it grounded."

"For now," Iris said with a smirk. "Give it a few hours, and they'll be calling it the 'fossil that rewrites history.'"

As if on cue, another voice chimed in, this time with exaggerated enthusiasm. "People are already asking—could this be evidence of species we never thought existed in this region? Could this change everything we know about prehistoric Europe?"

Reed switched off the radio with a flick of her fingers. "And there it is."

Iris huffed a small laugh. "Gotta love how fast they jump to conclusions."

Reed kept her eyes on the road. "That's why we're going to Professor Savas. We need facts, not headlines."

The conversation lulled as they drove on, the weight of the unknown settling between them.

✦ ✦ ✦

Professor Savas's Home

By the time they arrived, the sun had risen higher, casting warm light over the modest home. The house was tucked in a quiet neighborhood, a far cry from the bustling universities and lecture halls where Reed had once sat under Professor Savas's guidance.

The door opened before they even knocked.

Professor Daisy Savas stood in the doorway, her sharp eyes studying them both before breaking into a small, knowing smile. "Well, if it isn't Olivia Reed. You always did bring trouble with you."

Reed chuckled, stepping forward to greet her. "Good to see you too, Professor."

Daisy smiled softly, a touch of warmth in her eyes. "Well, I'm retired, but being called 'Professor' again by an old student always brings a little joy."

Iris extended a hand. "Iris, her unfortunate assistant."

Daisy shook her hand, amused. "Unfortunate, huh? You must have figured out by now that Reed drags people into all sorts of messes."

Iris grinned. "Oh, I'm getting there."

Daisy stepped aside, gesturing them in. "Alex is in his study. He's been digging through his collection since you called."

Reed exchanged a glance with Iris before following Daisy inside.

As Reed and Iris stepped inside, Daisy turned to Reed with a gentle smile. "How's Becca? I haven't spoken to her in so long."

Reed's expression softened. "She's doing well. She left paleontology after Dad's accident, but she's found something she loves."

Daisy nodded knowingly. "I remember how hard that was on her. How's Becca been holding up these days?"

"She teaches piano to little kids at home," Reed said. "It keeps her busy, and honestly, it makes both my parents happy."

Daisy's face brightened. "Piano? That's wonderful. I never imagined Becca trading fieldwork for sheet music, but if it brings her joy, that's what matters."

Reed smiled. "Yeah, I think she's finally at peace with it."

Daisy patted her arm warmly before leading them further inside.

The study was exactly how Reed remembered it—bookshelves overflowing, old papers stacked in precarious piles, the scent of aged pages lingering in the air. But now, the floor was littered with open books, scattered notes, and crinkled newspaper clippings.

Professor Alexander Savas stood near his desk, flipping through a heavy, leather-bound volume. He looked up as they entered, his expression unreadable.

"You're early," he noted, closing the book with a quiet thud.

Reed raised an eyebrow. "And you've been busy."

He gestured to the chaos around him. "Didn't take long to realize this wasn't just any discovery."

Daisy appeared at the doorway and gave her husband a pointed look. "And you, don't get lost in your books and forget there are living people in the room."

Savas smirked. "No promises."

Reed pulled out a chair, her eyes drifting over the scattered research. "Looks like you've been at this for a while," she remarked, her voice softening with admiration.

Professor Savas shrugged, a wry smile tugging at his lips. "I don't sleep much these days. When something piques my interest, I go all in." He gestured to the mess around them. "Thought I might find something that connects the dots. So far, it's mostly speculation."

Iris stepped closer, eyeing the pages and notes strewn around. "Do you think there's a connection between the bottle we found and the fossil?"

Savas sighed, leaning back in his chair as he adjusted his glasses. "That's the question, isn't it? The timeline doesn't add up. A modern bottle buried under thousands of years of sediment, and now a fossil from a time when it shouldn't be here... It's a puzzle."

Professor Daisy returned a few moments later, balancing a tray of teacups and a steaming pot. "You three have your theories to chase. I'll make sure you don't forget to drink something while you do." She set the tray down with a knowing smile. "I swear, the two of you together were always a disaster waiting to happen. Now you've dragged poor Iris into it."

Iris smirked, taking a sip from the cup of tea in her hand. "Oh, I walked into this willingly."

Daisy arched an eyebrow. "That just makes you more dangerous."

Reed chuckled before turning to Savas. "Did you find anything?"

Savas sighed, rubbing his temple as he looked over the mess of books and papers. "Not yet. I've been combing through some research papers, but nothing concrete so far." He flipped through a brittle page, frowning. "If this fossil is as out of place as it seems, we might be dealing with something completely undocumented."

Professor Daisy picked up a book herself, adjusting her glasses as she settled into a chair. "No known dinosaur species match the description of what came out of that crack." She scanned a passage before glancing at Savas. "Which means you're either looking in the wrong place or…" she trailed off, her lips quirking slightly, "you're looking for the wrong thing."

Savas rolled his eyes. "Here we go."

Reed pulled a folder from her bag and handed it to Professor Savas. "Before we get too deep into theories, take a look at this, Professor."

Savas opened it, his eyes narrowing as he scanned the test results from the bottle they had excavated. He flipped through the pages again as if expecting the numbers to change. "Three thousand years?" He exhaled sharply. "This is impossible."

Professor Daisy leaned forward, intrigued. "Let me see that." She took the papers, adjusting her glasses as she studied the results. Her brow furrowed before she reached for her phone. "I know someone who might have more insight on that fossil."

The room fell silent as Daisy made a quick call to one of her former students—one of the brightest in her field. They listened as she explained the situation, asking if there was any precedent for such a discovery in Greece.

When she hung up, she shook her head. "As expected, no known dinosaurs should be here. The geology just doesn't support it."

Reed crossed her arms. "So, we're back to square one."

Professor Daisy, however, didn't look discouraged. Instead, she stood and made her way to one of the tall bookshelves. "Maybe you're looking for something that never existed in the first place." She ran her fingers over the spines before pulling out an old volume on Greek mythology.

Savas groaned. "Daisy, we are looking for facts, not fairy tales."

Professor Daisy ignored him, flipping through the pages with a sharp focus. "Myths often have roots in something real," she mused.

Reed leaned closer, her curiosity piqued. "What are you thinking?"

Professor Daisy continued, "I am a paleontologist, but also a believer."

Professor Daisy stopped on a page, tapping a passage. "The Pyracmon."

Reed's eyes scanned the illustration—the lion's head, the human's body, the claws. She glanced at Daisy, then at Savas, who looked wholly unimpressed.

Savas rubbed his forehead. "You can't be serious."

But Reed wasn't so quick to dismiss it. "What if this isn't just a coincidence?" She turned back to the book, something clicking into place.

Iris, silent until now, looked between them. "You're saying… what? That the earthquake didn't just unearth a fossil, but a legend?"

Professor Daisy took a slow sip of tea, her expression thoughtful. "I'm saying maybe the two aren't so different."

Reed exhaled, staring at the pages. "Maybe, just maybe, the past wasn't as set in stone as they thought."

Professor Savas let out a slow breath, shaking his head. "You're telling me we should entertain the idea that what came out of that fissure is the remains of a mythological creature?"

Reed stared at the illustration of the Pyracmon, her fingers tracing the faded ink. "The thing is… myths don't just appear out of nowhere. They start somewhere, right?" She glanced up at Professor Savas, "Even if the fossil isn't a dinosaur, what if it's something else? Something that inspired the myth?"

Professor Savas crossed his arms. "Like what? An undiscovered species?"

"Maybe." Reed looked at Professor Daisy. "Or maybe something people weren't supposed to find."

Professor Daisy's lips curled into a knowing smile. "Now you're thinking."

Iris leaned back in her chair, "Okay, so let's say—for argument's sake—that this fossil is something unknown. If it's not a dinosaur, and it doesn't match any other known species, then what do we do next?"

Reed tapped the book thoughtfully. "We start by looking deeper into the Pyracmon myth. If there's even a sliver of truth behind it, then maybe—just maybe—there's more to this discovery than we realize."

Savas still looked skeptical but didn't argue. Instead, he exhaled sharply and moved to one of the cluttered bookshelves. "If we're going to do this, then we need more than just mythological accounts. There have been ancient reports of creatures that defy classification. Let's see if we can find any references beyond just Greek mythology."

Professor Daisy nodded approvingly. "I'll reach out to a few old colleagues and see if they've encountered anything remotely similar."

Iris sighed, "So basically, we're diving headfirst into a mystery that neither science nor history can fully explain."

Reed smirked, grabbing her cup of tea. "Wouldn't be the first time."

Iris groaned. "Why do I feel like I'm going to regret this?"

Professor Daisy chuckled, flipping another page. "Because, my dear, you probably will."

The room fell into a comfortable silence as each of them focused on their own research, the weight of the discovery settling over them. They were on the edge of something—something bigger than any of them had anticipated.

And deep down, Reed knew there was no turning back now.

Iris, who had been jotting notes, tapped her pen against the notepad. "So, we're looking at this from every possible angle—science, history, and mythology. Do we even have a timeline for when the excavation team will be able to fully extract and examine the fossil?"

Professor Savas exhaled. "That depends on how stable the site is after the earthquake. If the structure is compromised, they'll prioritize safety over digging."

Reed frowned. "Which means we might not have access to the fossil for a while."

Professor Daisy smirked. "All the more reason to get ahead of this while we can."

Professor Daisy adjusted her glasses. "Not just Greek mythology. Similar hybrid creatures exist in Mesopotamian and Persian legends. Even ancient Chinese and Indian texts describe beasts that seem like unnatural fusions."

"I remember hearing stories about the Narasimha Avatar, part-lion and part-man, depicted in Hindu mythology," said Reed.

Iris frowned. "But myths are just that—myths. How does this connect to what was found in Delphi?"

Professor Daisy tapped the illustration. "Because if we assume for a moment that myth has some root in reality, then we have to ask—why were these creatures described in such detail? And why do they appear in places where, biologically speaking, they shouldn't exist?"

Professor Daisy flipped to another page, filled with text in ancient Greek. "I'm saying we should stop assuming everything that sounds impossible is just a fairy tale, fantasy or whatever we call it."

Savas shook his head, standing up from his chair. "You're assuming far too much. We need hard evidence before we jump to conclusions."

But Daisy wasn't backing down. "Evidence is tricky when you're dealing with things that don't fit into our neat little boxes, Alex. Sometimes, the clues lie in places you least expect."

Iris, still processing the idea, murmured, "What if we're not looking at it the right way? What if this 'creature' was part of a different ecosystem—a world that doesn't quite fit into the standard categories of biological classification?"

Professor Daisy smiled, clearly enjoying the puzzle.

The room fell silent again as each of them stared at the scattered notes and books, each piece of the puzzle seeming both familiar and alien at the same time.

Outside, the wind rustled the leaves of the trees in the yard, carrying with it the promise of something greater. Something beyond their understanding.

The heavy silence in the room was broken by the sharp ring of Professor Savas's phone. He frowned, adjusting his glasses as he pulled it from his pocket. The moment he saw the caller ID, his posture straightened.

"Excuse me," he muttered, stepping outside the study to answer.

"Professor Savas speaking."

Reed, Iris, and Daisy exchanged glances as he left the room.

A moment later, another stretch of silence was interrupted again as he reentered. "Sure. I'll be there in the morning." He ended the call, placing the phone face down on the desk.

For a brief moment, he stood still, as if gathering his thoughts. Then, he turned to them. "That was the Geological and Paleontological Research Division. They want me at the site."

Reed leaned forward. "To study the fossil?"

Savas nodded, rubbing his chin. "They're keeping the details vague, but it's big enough to get the higher-ups involved. They need specialists. I told them I'm bringing my own team."

Pointing to Reed and Iris, he said, "Pack light. We leave first thing in the morning."

Professor Daisy exhaled, her eyes reflecting a mix of concern and pride. "Be careful, Alex," she said softly. "This is bigger than any of you realize."

A brief silence followed before Savas began gathering the scattered books on his desk, his mind already elsewhere. "Get some rest," he said. "We have a long day ahead of us."

✦ ✦ ✦

Chapter Seven

Beyond the Veil

The early morning sun cast a golden glow over the quiet streets as Reed steered the car through the winding roads leading out of the city. The vehicle hummed steadily beneath her grip, the weight of their mission pressing down on the otherwise peaceful drive.

Professor Savas sat in the front seat, his fingers occasionally drumming against his knee. He had been quiet for most of the journey, his mind clearly preoccupied. Iris sat in the back, eyes darting between the scenery flashing past and the digital notes she had compiled overnight.

The road to Delphi stretched ahead, winding through rugged hills still blanketed in dust and debris left by the earthquake.

As they neared Delphi, the once-distant mountain ridges loomed closer, their jagged silhouettes dark against the brightening sky. The roads became narrower, cutting through rough, uneven terrain.

The moment they arrived, the scale of destruction was even more apparent. Sections of the terrain had crumbled, exposing layers of rock that had remained untouched for millennia. Temporary fencing had been set up around the zone where the fossil had been uncovered. A checkpoint loomed ahead, marked by temporary barricades. Reed slowed the car as they reached the entrance. A security officer, clad in a high-visibility vest, stepped forward, gesturing for them to stop.

Professor Savas, presenting the required documents, said, "Professor Alexander Savas, leading the paleontological team. These are my associates, Dr. Reed and Ms. Iris."

The officer scanned the papers, nodding before waving them through. "You're expected. You can park near the field tent ahead." Reed maneuvered the car past the barricades, the tires crunching against gravel as they pulled up near a large white tent. Around them, teams of researchers and government officials moved with controlled urgency. Equipment was being set up, ground-penetrating radar units deployed, and specialists gathered in small clusters, their voices hushed but intense.

They stepped out of the car, the morning air thick with dust and the scent of disturbed earth.

A man in his late forties, with neatly combed hair and a sharp gaze, approached them. He extended a hand. “Professor Savas,” the man greeted. “Dr. Georgios, Head of the Seismology Department. Thank you for coming on such short notice. The situation is... unprecedented.”

Savas shook his hand. “We appreciate the opportunity to examine the specimen.”

They were led past the clusters of researchers, deeper into the excavation area. As they approached, Iris sucked in a sharp breath.

The fossil lay partially unearthed, embedded in stone.

The skeletal structure was massive, unlike anything they had ever seen. The ribcage was unnervingly broad, built to house a beast that had once commanded its domain with terrifying force.

Reed crouched beside it, running a gloved hand over the fossilized remains. “This isn’t reptilian,” she murmured.

Savas knelt next to her, his fingers tracing the jagged remains of what seemed like horned protrusions along the skull. The elongated jaw, lined with sharp, predatory teeth, gave the impression of a lion, yet the structure was far too alien to fit any known classification. His gaze shifted to the limbs—massive, with curved claws built for ripping through prey. “The bone composition is dense—far denser than anything from this period. It's built for extreme endurance." His brow furrowed. "This thing was a predator. Doesn't belong to any species we've ever recorded," he said, his voice low.

A tense silence followed. The weight of the discovery pressed down on them all.

"We'll need samples tested immediately," Savas said, rising to his feet. "DNA analysis, radiocarbon dating, structural comparisons. I need to know what this is."

One of the officials hesitated before speaking. "We've already started initial tests. The results are... unusual."

Savas straightened. "Unusual how?"

He continued, "We've conducted Fourier-transform infrared spectroscopy (FTIR) and micro-CT scanning to assess mineral composition and structural density. The fossil shows an unusual ratio of hydroxyapatite and trace elements that don't match normal fossilization patterns."

Iris frowned. "This... this isn't normal, is it? Have you ever seen anything like this before?"

Reed crossed her arms, glancing at the remains. "Unless we're dealing with a completely different set of biological or environmental factors."

Savas adjusted his glasses, his brow furrowed in thought. "Could it have been exposed to extreme mineralization processes? Volcanic activity? Unique soil composition?"

Dr. Georgios, who had been listening intently, added, "Delphi does have geothermal activity, but not at levels that would explain this level of preservation in such a short time."

Savas exhaled. "We'll need more tests. I want a full spectroscopic analysis of the mineral composition of these bones. And check for any organic remnants that might still be preserved."

The official nodded. "Of course. But word is already spreading, and the government will be making a formal statement soon."

As the day wore on, more samples were collected, more tests were set in motion. Yet, the more they uncovered, the fewer answers they had.

✦ ✦ ✦

Shifting Paradigms

After days of testing and analysis, they were no closer to an answer. Reed sat at her desk inside the tent, scanning the latest reports as the constant hum of researchers filled the air. Despite all the data in front of her, an uneasy feeling gnawed at her—like they were circling around something important, but failing to grasp it.

Nearby, Savas stood in quiet discussion with a few government officials. Reed hesitated, then took a deep breath and pushed back from the desk. "Professor, we need to talk."

He looked over at her, eyebrows raised. Noticing the tension in her voice, he excused himself from the conversation and followed her outside. The cool evening breeze stirred the loose edges of the excavation site, carrying with it the faint scent of disturbed earth.

"Professor," Reed began carefully, "I know this might sound ridiculous, but I... I've been thinking about something Iris mentioned yesterday. We know this fossil is unlike anything we've seen before, but after reviewing the data, it feels like we're missing something. Something more than just biological." She hesitated, then pushed forward. "I think we need to consider what Professor Daisy said."

Savas exhaled sharply, pinching the bridge of his nose. "Reed, I respect Daisy immensely, but we're talking about science. Mythological creatures are just that—myths."

Reed crossed her arms. "What else could it be? Because right now, we have a massive, fossilized creature that defies classification, with no evolutionary history to trace it back to."

Savas remained quiet, reluctant.

Reed took a deep breath. "Look, Professor, we have to consider every possibility. What if—just hear me out—this isn't from Earth? What if we're dealing with an extraterrestrial species?"

Savas frowned, thoughtful. "I won't dismiss the possibility outright. We know microbial life could exist elsewhere, maybe even more complex organisms. But Reed, if this were alien, where's the evidence of how it got here? There's no impact crater, no spacecraft debris, nothing to suggest an extraterrestrial arrival. We expanded the search radius, scanned the terrain—there's nothing."

"That's exactly my point," Reed countered. "If it didn't come from another planet, then maybe it came from our own past. Mythology isn't just stories, Professor. Think about it—ancient civilizations recorded what they believed to be real. What if they weren't just imagining monsters? What if they were remembering something? Creatures that walked the earth long before recorded history."

Savas stared at her, silent.

Reed took a step closer. "Just call her. Tell her the latest results. See what she thinks."

He let out a sigh, pulling out his phone.

As he dialed, he gave Reed a long, uncertain look. "Mythology? Reed, we've been over this. What you're suggesting is—"

"I know it sounds crazy," she cut in, her voice firm, "but given the evidence, we can't ignore the possibility. What if it isn't just a fossil of an unknown species? What if it's connected to something from the past—something mythical?"

After a few rings, Daisy picked up, sounding both eager and apprehensive. "Alex! Hey, you good?"

"Hi, yeah, I'm good," the professor sighed.

Daisy continued with an eagerness in her voice. "You never call me from the field. What's wrong?"

Savas hesitated, his thoughts circling around Reed's words. "It's... interesting. But there's something you should know. Reed suggested something I never thought I'd even consider. She's been looking over the fossil findings, and she's... well, she's wondering if there's more to this than just science. Something... mythological."

There was a long pause on the other end, and Savas could almost hear Daisy's sharp intake of breath.

"You were right to question things," he admitted. "The skull—it's leonine but has two horns. The body is... disturbingly human-like. And the mineralization, nothing makes sense."

Another silence, heavy with thought.

When Daisy spoke again, her voice was steady but urgent. "Alex, listen to me. You need to contact Professor Arthur Blackwood from the Mythology Studies Department at the Institute of Classical Studies and Mythology. He's spent his entire career analyzing ancient texts that reference creatures believed to be fictional. If there's any historical account of something like this, he'll know."

Savas pressed his fingers against his temple. "Daisy, do you realize what you're suggesting? I can't just walk up to the higher-ups and tell them we need a mythologist."

"Then don't," she shot back. "Tell them you need a cultural historian. Frame it however you want, but if this thing has ties to recorded history—even in myth—wouldn't you want to know?"

He let out a slow breath, staring at the excavation site in the distance. The thought of consulting someone like Blackwood felt absurd... but so did the fossil itself.

Savas ran a hand through his graying hair, reluctantly accepting her thought.

Savas had been chewing on Daisy's words all night, and by morning, the internal conflict had turned into something more pressing. He struggled with how to present the possibility of mythology being linked to the fossil to the higher-ups. The idea seemed too outlandish, too speculative, but he couldn't shake the feeling that something more was at play.

He walked through the excavation site, the morning air thick with dust and earth. Inside one of the larger tents, he found Dr. Georgios hunched over a table cluttered with reports and test findings. He looked up as Savas entered, eyes weary yet sharp.

"Professor Savas," Georgios greeted, setting down his pen. "You look like a man with something on his mind."

Savas took a deep breath and pulled up a chair. "You could say that. I need your help with something."

Georgios gave him a wary look. "That sounds ominous."

Savas hesitated before choosing his words carefully. "I know how this is going to sound, but hear me out. We've exhausted every scientific avenue, and nothing adds up. The fossil—its structure, its mineralization—doesn't fit into any known category. We need to start thinking outside the box."

Georgios folded his arms. "Go on."

Savas continued, "We're looking at something that defies classification. If there's a historical precedent, we can't ignore it."

After a few seconds of silence, he continued, "Professor Arthur Blackwood, an expert from the Institute of Classical Studies and Mythology, has spent years analyzing ancient texts that reference creatures believed to be fictional. If there's anything remotely similar to what we've uncovered, he'll be the one to know."

Georgios was quiet for a long time before exhaling sharply. "This is insane," he muttered. But then he leaned back, considering. "You said Professor Arthur Blackwood? Now that's a name I haven't heard in a while."

Savas raised an eyebrow. "You know him?"

"Never met personally," Georgios admitted, "but I've followed his work. The man is brilliant—one of the few scholars who can navigate both myth and history without losing his credibility."

But then, to Savas' surprise, he continued, "I'll try. First, let me make some calls."

After a few calls and a handful of diplomatic maneuvers, Georgios managed to get in touch with Professor Blackwood through the university's connections.

By evening, after securing confirmation from Professor Blackwood, Dr. Georgios gathered Professor Savas, Dr. Reed, and a few other officials and researchers at the site. As he stepped into the tent, he glanced around at the expectant faces before addressing them.

"Professor Savas came up with an interesting thought this morning," Georgios began. "Since we've failed to classify the fossil within any known category of the animal kingdom, he suggested we consider the possibility that we might be dealing with something believed to be myth or fiction. After careful consideration and pulling some strings, we're bringing in Professor Arthur Blackwood, a mythologist from the Institute of Classical Studies and Mythology."

A murmur passed through the group, some exchanging uncertain glances while others leaned in with intrigue.

"He's in Seville," Georgios continued. "Delivering a lecture on Greek mythology. I was careful with my approach—explained that we have an unusual case, one that could benefit from his insight."

Professor Savas exhaled, the weight of uncertainty still lingering. "And?"

"He's intrigued," Georgios said. "He's already checking for the earliest available flight tomorrow."

A long silence settled over the group as the implications sank in. Just as they were about to disperse, Georgios spoke again, his tone firm.

"This stays between us. If word gets out that we're bringing in a mythologist to consult on a paleontological discovery, it'll raise questions we're not prepared to answer."

Meanwhile…

Media is always the media, constantly chasing sensational stories to skyrocket their TRP ratings. As the Delphi discovery continued making waves, news outlets found their next distraction—shifting public attention by fixating on a celebrity's personal life. With people always eager for gossip, the headlines moved away from science and archeology, diving into speculation and controversy surrounding the latest scandal. Reporters, desperate to maintain momentum, blended fact with fiction to keep audiences hooked.

✦ ✦ ✦

Chapter Eight

"Life Isn't Always Black and White"

A gust of warm wind swept across the excavation site as the first rays of morning light cast long shadows over the tents. A car rumbled to a stop near the entrance, and as the door opened, Professor Arthur Blackwood stepped out. A man in his late fifties or early sixties, he carried himself with quiet authority, his salt-and-pepper hair neatly combed back, sharp eyes framed by rectangular spectacles with an eyeglass chain resting against his collar. His attire reflected both scholarly refinement and practicality: a well-fitted dark blazer over a crisp white shirt, paired with charcoal trousers and sturdy leather shoes, suited for both lecture halls and rugged terrain. Over one shoulder, he carried a worn leather bag, the kind that had seen years of travel, filled with notes, books, and knowledge passed through generations.

Standing nearby, Dr. Georgios, who oversaw the excavation, approached with Professor Savas to welcome him.

"Professor Blackwood," Georgios greeted, extending a firm handshake. "I appreciate you making the trip on such short notice."

Blackwood offered a small, knowing smile. "When an archeologist or paleontologist calls a mythologist, it usually means something doesn't quite fit the conventional explanations. I was intrigued."

"Then you'll find this even more intriguing," Savas remarked, as he gestured toward the research tent.

Inside, under the dim glow of desk lamps, reports, test results, and high-resolution scans of the fossil were spread across a table. Blackwood removed his blazer, draped it over a chair, and adjusted his spectacles before carefully examining the documents. His fingers traced over mineral analysis reports, radiocarbon dating results, and anatomical reconstructions of the fossil. The room remained silent as he processed the data, occasionally nodding or furrowing his brow.

After a few minutes, he reached into his bag and retrieved two items—a leather-bound notebook filled with years of personal notes and an aged, torn book, its pages yellowed with time. The title, barely legible, referenced ancient legends of Delphi. Flipping through the fragile pages, he scanned passages with intense focus, occasionally cross-referencing them with his own notes.

Finally, he stepped toward the fossil itself. Blackwood observed it closely, circling the preserved remains, tilting his head as he analyzed the unusual features. He leaned in, adjusting his glasses, his expression unreadable. He examined the skull structure, the faint traces of what appeared to be horn-like protrusions, the unsettling blend of humanoid and animalistic traits.

After a long pause, he pulled out his notebook again and began writing on a fresh page, his pen scratching softly against the paper. Then, under his breath, he murmured a single word.

"Pyracmon…"

Savas, standing nearby, caught the sound but not the meaning. "What?" he asked, leaning in.

Blackwood straightened, turning toward the others in the tent. His expression was thoughtful, his voice steady.

"I believe you've uncovered something far older than the myth itself," he said. "A legend nearly lost to time. Let me tell you about Pyracmon."

A charged silence filled the tent, the air thick with anticipation. Blackwood's reputation preceded him—he was not one to make careless claims. An astute scholar, his meticulous research and sharp instincts had rarely, if ever, led him astray. And now, standing before them, his gaze unwavering, he was about to unearth a truth buried deeper than time itself.

He placed his hand on the worn cover of the ancient book he had brought, its spine barely holding together. "Unlike the well-documented creatures of Greek mythology—the Minotaur, Medusa, the Chimera—there are only the faintest whispers of Pyracmon." His fingers traced a faded line of text as he continued, "The existence of such a being was mentioned so briefly, so inconsistently, that most scholars dismissed it as nothing more than an embellishment in fragmented texts."

He glanced up, making eye contact with each of them before flipping to another page, where ink had bled into the fragile parchment. "But I never dismissed it." He reached for his leather-bound notebook, thick with years of collected theories, annotations, and cross-references. "For decades, I have gathered remnants of forgotten myths—patterns that elude mainstream academia. Pyracmon was one such anomaly, a legend so elusive it seemed almost as if someone had deliberately erased its place in history."

He paused, letting the weight of his words settle. Then, tapping on the anatomical sketches spread across the table, he said, "And yet, here we are, standing before something that defies classification—something that should not exist. But it does."

The flickering lamplight cast shadows across his face as he continued, his voice quieter but no less certain. "If the past has taught us anything, it's that myths are often built upon truths, however distorted they may become over time. Pyracmon was said to have stood in the path of the Helios Prism, guarding a passage that few dared to cross."

He paused for a moment. "The Helios Prism... it's mentioned in a handful of obscure texts—often as a metaphor, sometimes as an object of divine light. Some believed it symbolized enlightenment, others thought it literal."

He gestured to the fossil again. "And now, we may be looking at the evidence that it was never just a myth to begin with."

He paused, his gaze sweeping across the room. "But there's more to this than just a guardian lost to time." He tapped his fingers against the aged book in front of him. "Legends spoke of Pyracmon's purpose—not merely as a sentry, but as a test. It remained at the threshold of the Prism until one deemed worthy arrived. Only then would it relinquish its watch."

Blackwood exhaled slowly, his fingers tightening slightly over the edge of his notebook. "So, if Pyracmon is here; its remains uncovered after centuries—then the Helios Prism itself is no longer waiting to be claimed." His voice dropped to a near whisper. "It is already in the hands of someone the past would call… worthy."

A hush fell over the tent. Even the rustling of papers and the occasional distant voices from the excavation site seemed to fade into nothingness.

Iris glanced nervously at the others, her voice barely audible. "You mean... someone has already found it?"

Dr. Georgios looked stunned, his earlier skepticism shaken.

Savas exhaled, breaking the silence. "So, all those stories... they weren't just allegory?"

Blackwood closed his notebook with a decisive snap. "I am saying," he replied, "that history may have just rewritten itself."

✦ ✦ ✦

Chapter Nine

An Ancient Trial

Back in the Past in Ancient Delphi…

Mira and her team were utterly drained after their narrow escape from Pyracmon. Bruised, soot-streaked, and still catching their breath, they moved in silence through the aftermath of the battle, each step heavier than the last. But even in their exhaustion, the Oracle's words lingered—echoing not just as warnings, but as messages shaped unnervingly for each of them. The trials she had cautioned them about no longer seemed like vague prophecies but rather pronouncements tailored specifically to them.

They found themselves stumbling into a quiet glade. It was a quiet place, seemingly untouched by chaos, yet humming with presence. Towering trees encircled the clearing like ancient guardians, their branches high and wide like outstretched arms ready to shield or strike. A breeze rustled their leaves with a hush so soft it sounded like whispers. At the center stood a stone archway, worn by time yet still proud in its posture. Most of its surfaces were carved with depictions of the sun, its rays, and other designs, all of which were attributes of Helios and appeared to be remnants of antiquity. The atmosphere around them was heavy and alight with electrical sensations that were both eerie and irresistible.

Nikos stopped abruptly, his eyes locking with Mira's. "This is where I leave you," he said, his voice tight. He touched the wall beside him, then added in a near whisper, "Every step forward costs something." Before she could speak, he turned and vanished into the mist.

Mira experienced a shift in perception as they stepped through the arch. It was almost as if they had entered a different realm. The world behind her faded into silence. Ahead of them stretched a vast, labyrinthine structure. From above, it might have resembled a great sun, its rays spreading across the forest floor in chaotic patterns. The maze was made of ancient stones, moss-covered and cracked, but still emanating a quiet grandeur. There was no path that seemed more correct than another—each one turned and twisted, inviting them with equal mystery. Etched into the stone beside the entrance was an inscription:

> ***Only those who walk in wisdom and harmony shall treasure the light they seek.***

The more Mira's team delved into the labyrinth, the more they felt the dense atmosphere charged with ancient energy. A subtle hum seemed to rise from the ground itself, vibrating in the soles of their feet. The walls, though rough-hewn, occasionally glinted with mineral threads that caught shafts of light from cracks above. The team walked cautiously, their footsteps echoing softly against the ancient stone. Beams of sunlight streamed occasionally through small cracks above, casting shifting patterns of light and shadow that seemed to dance across the walls. Occasionally, they could feel the shadows move on their own, as if watching their every step. Each path offered new opportunities as they explored, leading them into different chambers, all of which were built to challenge their strength, intellect, and determination in unimaginable ways.

Their first challenge lay ahead of them in a circular chamber where slender shafts of light streamed through high windows and onto the ground where stones were engraved with various symbols. Each of these symbols was associated with one of the three aspects of Helios; the first one was the sun; the second was time and the last one was the guardian of wisdom. On the wall, an inscription read:

> ***To harness the light, the wise must cast no shadow. Step into the path where the sun's truth flows unbroken.***

Mira and her team attempted to decode the riddle. She took a step forward as it dawned on her that light symbolized clarity, while a shadow meant hesitation or doubt clouding one's judgment. She held her breath, waiting for her heart to steady. Then, she stepped forward, adjusting her posture to keep within the beam of pure sunlight. Her movements were slow and deliberate, every motion controlled. Even the flicker of her cloak threatened to betray her with a wisp of shadow. But she held her course. The air around her seemed to shimmer with intensity. The light flickered, testing her poise, forcing her to steady her focus. After a tense moment, just as her foot touched the final stone, the room brightened, illuminating a new path as a reward for her resolve and clarity as a leader. Her team followed, encouraged by her success.

Deeper in the maze, they arrived in a room of mirrors. The glass was ancient but unblemished, perfectly reflecting their images. Rays of sunlight fell on the mirrors, casting beams of light that illuminated five different passages.

Each of them felt irresistibly drawn toward one of the paths. There was no discussion; something instinctual was guiding them. Josh moved first, drawn like iron to a magnet, followed by Jasper, Annie, Tony, and finally Mira—each to the path marked for them.

✦ ✦ ✦

Annie's trial of creativity:

Annie's impetuous enthusiasm for both Greek mythology and Art swept her into a room quite obviously designed to test her ability to see connections where others might not. The room was lined up with statues of mythological beings in different elaborate poses, with intricate facial expressions, and the walls were painted with scenes from various myths, though parts were incomplete, left in the shadow. On the east side of the room was a very large black wall, surrounded by ancient pigments and brushes scattered around it. The inlay read:

> ***Bring to life the stories that lie in the shadow.***

A strange restlessness settled in her fingertips. She understood immediately—this was not just a test of memory, but of connection. In order for the door to unlock itself, Annie had to finish the mural. She had to fill in those missing pieces by connecting the myths represented in the room. It required not only an understanding of history but also vision.

She knew that each of the statues she possessed held the key to its story, and when she examined them, fragments of each tale sprang to her mind. Connecting all the figures into one solid story, Annie used her imagination and deep knowledge of mythology to paint one seamless scene. As she added the final stroke, the room glowed with bright light, and the door opened, rewarding her ability to connect art, myth, and story with a joyful, creative spirit.

✦ ✦ ✦

Jasper's trial of knowledge:

In the dark chamber with old writings on the walls, Jasper, a reserved but sharp-eyed scholar with a Ph.D. in ancient languages, faced a challenge that shook him to his core. The writing on the wall comprised Latin and ancient Greek. However, most of this writing had been weathered beyond recognition over time. Ahead of him lay a stone path with large, movable slabs, each engraved with phrases from different texts. Some were riddles, some verses, some fragments of epics long lost. The inscription above read:

> ***Rebuild the truth hidden by time.***

Jasper's heart thumped. This was his domain—but the stakes were real. He had to put the slabs in the correct sequence to complete the broken passage on the wall. Each time a slab was placed correctly, the sentence on the wall briefly glowed, revealing the entire inscription. With each failed attempt, however, the chamber tightened, walls creeping closer, stone crushing beneath his feet, as if urging him to speed up. Sweat clung to his temple as he muttered translations, debated grammatical structure, and squinted at the faded text. Jasper calmed himself, took a deep breath and then carefully analyzed each phrase, relying on his knowledge to identify missing words and reconstruct the texts. As he completed the final sentence, the entire chamber lit up, and the path ahead solidified, rewarding his ability to trust his knowledge and remain steady under pressure.

✦ ✦ ✦

Josh's trial of patience:

Josh, Mira's sarcastic but talented student, entered a chamber that challenged him to put aside his wit and confront a task requiring patience and focus. The room contained a massive sundial that cast shadows on various symbols etched along the walls. The shadows shifted rapidly, flickering in and out of alignment. An inscription read:

> ***To master the shadow, one must still the mind.***

The only way to unlock the door was to align each symbol with the sundial's shadow precisely, but the faster he moved, the faster the symbols spun out of place. Josh, typically quick to make a joke or react impulsively, had to resist the urge to rush through the task. Frustration built as he tried to steady the sundial, but he realized that only by slowing down and focusing fully on each move could he align the symbols correctly. For someone used to clever solutions, this felt like a punishment.

He sat. Took a breath. Closed his eyes.

As he calmed his mind and steadied his hands, he gradually brought each shadow into alignment, proving his ability to set aside his ego and find discipline. Each motion became a meditation. With deliberate focus, he adjusted the dial, breathing in rhythm. It took time—more than he liked—but finally, the last shadow slid into place, perfectly aligned. The chamber unlocked, acknowledging his growth in humility and focus.

He grinned. "Maybe patience is a virtue," he muttered.

✦ ✦ ✦

Tony's trial of strength and focus:

Tony, known for his steady presence and determination, stepped into a chamber filled with intricate mechanical devices and levers set into the walls. Each device was connected to a series of stone doors along the far wall, and above them, an inscription read:

> ***Only those who persevere may find the true path.***

The challenge lay not in brute strength, but in careful observation and resilience. Tony had to pull the levers in a precise sequence to open the correct door, but there was a twist—each time he pulled the wrong lever, the room reset with a loud, grinding sound, closing all doors and dimming the lights. The challenge wasn't in brute strength—it was in resilience. In enduring failure and continuing without falter. To succeed, Tony had to keep track of each lever and its effect on the doors, learning from each failed attempt and pressing forward without letting frustration cloud his focus. After several resets, Tony began to see patterns in the mechanisms, allowing him to deduce the correct sequence. Some levers triggered multiple mechanisms. Some were decoys. Tony began keeping count, mentally mapping the room. With every reset, his strategy refined. With each correct pull, the doors gradually opened one by one, leading him closer to the exit. Finally, as he pulled the last lever in the sequence, the final door swung open, and the room filled with light, rewarding Tony's resilience, patience, and keen attention to detail.

✦ ✦ ✦

Mira's trial of balance:

Mira entered a vast, circular chamber, the walls lined with intricate celestial dials. On opposite walls, two pedestals stood—each with a large dial that represented either dawn or dusk. The dial on the left was bathed in soft, golden hues, symbolizing dawn, while the dial on the right glowed with the warm purples and reds of sunset, symbolizing dusk. At the center of the room was an inscription:

> ***To lead, one must balance the new dawn and the fading dusk. Find harmony between the two, and the path will open.***

Mira understood this deeply. Leadership wasn't one extreme or another—it was walking the line between them. One dial represented hope and beginnings. The other, endings and wisdom.

Mira had to rotate both dials to a precise position—one that symbolized balance, where the light of dawn and the colors of dusk complemented each other. However, the trial was not straightforward. When she adjusted one dial, the other slowly began to shift back to its original position. To succeed, Mira had to adjust the first dial slightly ahead of the correct balance point, so that by the time she reached the second dial and adjusted it, the first dial would have naturally returned to the perfect position. Mira tried several times, the task proving more difficult with each attempt. Each time she reached the second pedestal; she found that the first dial had moved from its position. But with each failure, Mira learned more about the necessary timing and the slight adjustments needed to make the two dials align perfectly. Finally, after many attempts, Mira adjusted the first dial just enough, then hurried to the second pedestal, finding the perfect balance between dawn and dusk. As both dials aligned perfectly, the room filled with a soft, harmonious light. The door ahead opened, rewarding her for her patience, timing, and ability to balance the new beginnings of dawn with the reflective wisdom of dusk.

✦ ✦ ✦

Chapter Ten

Final Challenge - The Hourglass and The Helios Prism

After completing their individual trials, Mira and her team had found themselves standing together once more, united yet changed by the challenges they had endured. The air was thick with anticipation, charged with the hum of ancient energy that seemed to ripple through the walls of the grand chamber. It was vast and circular, with towering pillars engraved with celestial patterns—constellations, solar flares, and mythical symbols spiraling toward a domed ceiling where a mosaic of Helios driving his chariot blazed in hues of gold and crimson.

At the eastern end of the chamber, a faint glowing spot shimmered on the wall, its light pulsating softly like the first rays of dawn. The symbol of the sunrise—a promise of hope, renewal, and the endless cycle of beginnings and endings. There, embedded in the wall, was a small concave dip, its dimensions perfectly proportioned for the hourglass they had discovered during their excavation at the beginning of their expedition.

Mira pulled out the hourglass from her backpack. Its surface, though ancient, gleamed as if freshly polished, the sands within swirling with flecks of light that shimmered like trapped stars. As she moved closer, her heart pounded with a sense of purpose, and the weight of the hourglass felt different now—heavier, as if it contained not just sand, but echoes of their journey, every trial and triumph condensed into grains of time.

With a steady breath, Mira placed the hourglass into the wall indentation. A quiet, resonant click reverberated through the chamber, sending tremors along the floor and causing the celestial engravings on the walls to glow faintly. She stepped back, eyes wide with wonder.

The click was followed by a low hum that grew in intensity, vibrating through their bones. A deep, resounding echo spread across the chamber, like a heartbeat pulsing through the very stone. Then, slowly, a mechanism within the wall began to shift, ancient gears groaning to life. Dust fell from unseen crevices, and a golden latch slid away, revealing the Helios Prism, held in place by an ornate clip.

As the latch released, the Prism floated gently, suspended in midair, and began to rotate slowly, casting shards of light across the chamber. The shimmering beams refracted off the stone walls, painting symbols and patterns that rippled and shifted like living constellations. A low hum vibrated through the room, resonating in their bones, as if the chamber itself were awakening after centuries of slumber.

Mira's breath caught as the light enveloped her. It was warm—not just in temperature, but in sensation—like sunlight distilled into its purest essence. Her fingers tingled, and a soft whisper, almost imperceptible, danced at the edge of her consciousness. She blinked, and the world around her vanished.

She was standing beneath a vast expanse of sky that blazed with hues of gold and crimson. The sun hung low on the horizon, impossibly large and radiating with a power that felt ancient and omniscient. The ground beneath her feet was not stone but fine, glittering sand that shimmered with each shift of the wind. Mira turned slowly, her eyes widening as she took in the landscape: towering temples with spires that pierced the heavens, their surfaces carved with intricate designs of suns, lotuses, and swirling fire.

Massive statues of gods and celestial beings lined the paths, their eyes cast eternally skyward.

A river, broad and glittering like molten gold, snaked through the land, its waters reflecting the brilliance of the sun above. Along its banks, vibrant flowers bloomed in colors she had never seen—deep indigos, blazing oranges, and shimmering golds that seemed to pulse with life. And towering above it all, at the very heart of the landscape, stood a grand temple crowned with a dome of pure light. Its spire reached into the sky, entwined with vines of gold and symbols that shimmered and shifted as if alive.

Mira felt a pull, gentle yet undeniable, drawing her closer to the temple. She took a step forward, and the whisper grew louder—a language she didn't recognize but somehow understood. It spoke of light and time, of destiny entwined with the sun's eternal path. As she approached, the doors of the temple—enormous and etched with symbols of the sun god—began to part with a whisper of wind.

Her hand stretched out, fingertips grazing the surface of the light that poured from within. And then, with a rush of warmth and sound, the vision shattered.

Mira gasped, stumbling backward. She was back in the chamber, the Prism still rotating slowly, its light dancing across the walls. Her heart pounded wildly, and her hands shook with the echo of that warmth. She looked around, her team staring at her with puzzled expressions, their brows furrowed.

"What happened?" Mira began, her voice unsteady.

Tony replied, "You just kind of...stopped for a few seconds. Stared at it like you were frozen."

Mira blinked, her hands still tingling. "No...it was longer. I saw...I saw a place. A temple—massive, with symbols of the sun god everywhere. It felt...alive. And the light, it was...it was like it was calling me."

Annie stepped closer, concern flickering in her eyes. "Are you sure? It was just a moment, hardly thirty seconds."

Mira shook her head firmly. "No, it wasn't a dream. I was there, a distant world full of exotic landscapes and ancient symbols. I felt the sand beneath my feet. I heard the river...saw the temple. It was real." Her gaze dropped to the Prism, still suspended midair, its glow softer now, as if resting. "It showed me something. Something I think we need to find."

A silence settled over the group, heavy with disbelief and awe. Finally, Jasper cleared his throat. "If that's true...then the Helios Prism is more than just a key. It's a map. Or maybe...an invitation."

Mira looked back at the Prism, determination flaring in her eyes. “It wants us to follow it.”

The Prism, as if responding to her words, pulsed gently, its light flickering with the intensity of a heartbeat.

The Helios Prism hovered for a moment longer, rotating gracefully, casting fractured light across the chamber’s ancient walls. Its glow softened, almost like a sigh, before descending gently into Mira’s waiting hands. She cradled it carefully, its surface warm against her palms. For a heartbeat, the room fell silent, and the air grew still as if the very stones were holding their breath.

A soft rumble broke the silence, low and resonant, vibrating through the floor beneath their feet. At the far end of the chamber, where the shadows had been thickest, stone ground against stone. Dust spilled from the cracks as a hidden door, narrow and unassuming, began to slide open.

Golden light streamed through the gap, growing brighter as the door widened. Sunlight—pure and unfiltered—spilled into the chamber, illuminating the swirling patterns carved into the walls and catching flecks of dust that danced in the air. It was as though dawn itself had pierced the ancient stone to beckon them forward.

Tony squinted, shielding his eyes from the sudden brightness. “Is that…?”

Mira nodded, eyes wide with awe. "Sunlight."

Without another word, Tony stepped forward, his steps echoing on the stone floor as he approached the doorway. He paused at its threshold, glancing back at the others with a grin that was equal parts disbelief and exhilaration. "Coming?"

Josh followed, then Jasper, his eyes scanning the symbols on the walls one last time before stepping through. Annie went next, her hand brushing the stone frame as she passed. Finally, Mira moved forward, the Helios Prism still pulsing gently in her grasp. She took a deep breath and stepped through the doorway.

The moment Mira crossed the threshold, sunlight struck the surface of the Prism with startling intensity. A brilliant flash of light erupted, enveloping them all in a blinding warmth. It wasn't harsh; it was soothing, like stepping into the embrace of a midsummer sun. The light grew brighter, flooding their senses until the world around them dissolved into pure radiance.

Mira felt weightless, suspended in that golden glow. She couldn't see her team, but she felt them—like flickers of warmth dancing beside her, tethered together by the journey they had just survived. The sensation lasted for only a moment, but within it, time stretched and folded, as if centuries unraveled and stitched back together in the span of a heartbeat.

Then, with a sudden gasp, the light receded. Mira blinked rapidly, her vision adjusting to the stark contrast of muted light and shadow. The scent of damp earth and fresh rain filled her lungs. The familiar shapes of canvas tents and excavation equipment stretched out before her. Birds chirped overhead, their melodies mingling with the distant rumble of cars and the whisper of leaves.

They were back—right where it had all begun. The excavation site sprawled before them, untouched and unknowing of the passage of time. Sunlight glinted off metal tools, scattered across the ground where they had left them.

Tony staggered slightly, catching himself with a laugh. "We're...we're back."

Jasper's hand went to his head. "That was… did that really just happen?"

Annie laughed, almost breathless. "If it didn't, we all just had the most vivid hallucination of our lives."

Mira looked down at her hands, half-expecting the Helios Prism to be gone—but it wasn't. It rested in her palms, its light softer now, as if content with its journey. She turned it slowly, watching as the sunlight refracted off its surface, casting faint symbols onto the dirt below. Her heart thudded in her chest, heavy with the promise of what lay ahead.

✦ ✦ ✦

The Whispers of What's to Come

As the team gathered their bearings, Mira stepped away from the group, her eyes still fixed on the Prism. There was something different about it now—an energy humming just beneath its surface, waiting. She traced the smooth edges with her fingertips, feeling a pulse of warmth each time her hands brushed the engraved symbols.

A whisper, soft as a breath, slipped into her consciousness, threading through her thoughts like silk. It was not in words, but in feeling—an urge, a pull toward something distant and ancient. Mira closed her eyes, and for just a fraction of a second, she saw it again: towering temples, shimmering rivers, spires reaching for the heavens. The vision vanished as quickly as it had come, leaving her breathless.

"Mira?" Josh's voice snapped her back to the present. He stood a few feet away, brow raised. "You alright?"

Mira looked up, the Prism still warm in her hands. Her gaze turned, eyes narrowing at the horizon, where the sun dipped low, casting long shadows over the land. She knew this wasn't over. Whatever the Prism had shown her, it was real. And it was waiting.

"Yeah," she replied, her voice steady. "I'm more than alright." She met his eyes, a spark of determination igniting within her. "We've just begun."

And as the sunlight stretched across the excavation site, casting long, gilded paths over the earth, Mira held the Helios Prism a little tighter, knowing that its secrets had only just started to unfold.

-------------------**The End**-----------------